"An intrigu... ...od read."

CHRISTIAN WEEK

"Heavy on the intrigue, subtle with the theology, *The Search* is an enticing distraction."

NEW MAN

"*The Search* is an interesting, well-plotted story. I enjoyed the sharp characterizations reminiscent of Len Deighton. It's nice to see that a mystery novel can be constructed within a Christian perspective. Good stuff."

ST. CATHERINES, ONTARIO

"Badke avoids the usual extremes of Christian mystery writing, and the result is a good, though-provoking read."

MENNONITE BRETHREN HERALD

"Compelling adventure...Badke has successfully avoided the syrupy shallowness that has for so long given Christian fiction a bad name... *The Search* is a good read."

CHRISTIAN INFO NEWS

"*Saluso's Game* is a good, gut-grabbing mystery."

MARTHA SLEEPER,
DICK SLEEPER DISTRIBUTION

A BEN SYLVESTER MYSTERY

AVENGER

WILLIAM BADKE

MULTNOMAH BOOKS • SISTERS, OREGON

This book is a work of fiction, and all the characters in this novel are fictional. Any resemblance to actual persons, living or dead, is purely coincidental.

AVENGER

published by Multnomah Books
a part of the Questar publishing family

© 1997 by William Badke
International Standard Book Number: 1-57673-031-X

Cover Design by Kevin Keller
Cover Illustration by Tom Collicott
Edited by Rodney L. Morris

Printed in the United States of America

For information:
QUESTAR PUBLISHERS, INC.
POST OFFICE BOX 1720
SISTERS, OREGON 97759

LIBRARY OF CONGRESS CATALOGING-IN-PUBLICATION DATA
Badke, William B., 1949-
    Avenger/by William B. Badke.   p. cm.
    (A Ben Sylvester mystery; book 3)
    ISBN 1-57673-031-X (alk. paper) I. Title. II. Series: Badke, William
B., 1949- Ben Sylvester mystery; book 3.
PS3552.A318A94 1997   96-48707
813'.54--dc21   CIP

97 98 99 00 01 02 03 04 — 10 9 8 7 6 5 4 3 2 1

Avenger

I was staring at the boulevard, thinking how wide it was compared with the narrow alleys in the rest of the city, age-stained Spanish buildings radiating the heat of the sun across the four lanes and the flowered median, when my side mirror blew off and glass splattered all over the side of my car. Two heavy thumps somewhere in the back, and my right foot went down all by itself, the ancient Chevy lurching into a roar as I raced toward the end of the block and took the corner without braking.

Feeling my wheels lift off the ground as I turned and shot down the hill on the restricted side avenue lost in a canyon of buildings. Praying that no one would get in my way, weaving around a taxi, then clear sailing all the way to the bottom, where the squatters lived.

Slowing, I followed rambling alleys, turning often, checking the inside mirror for followers, seeing none. Not a one. It must have been a stationary sniper firing at me from a building, though it was beyond me how someone could have taken a rifle into a row of government offices.

Unless, of course, they had official status—police or counter-intelligence. Goodness knows I'd antagonized enough officials in the twenty-four hours since I'd flown into the country.

With growing certainty that no one was after me for the moment, I started to weigh my options, still driving my shabby rental as I explored the real city—the dwelling place of the poor. To be sure, I'd seen similar things in slums elsewhere, but it still amazed me how people could take paper and scraps of metal and twine and discarded plywood, and turn it all into a home. What with open sewers and rotten water supply, it was likely that few of their children ever lived to enjoy their environment.

Think. Someone just tried to kill you, so what do you do?

a. Pretend that it didn't happen and go about your business.

b. Go back angry to the chief of operations and demand to be protected.

c. Take the first flight home, leaving your luggage behind.

I was sick of Simpson dumping these really bad jobs on me. The guy seemed to take pleasure in knocking me off the rails. But this one was worse. I'd just come off six months of sick leave, and I was still using a cane because of the bullet damage from the last job he'd sent me on.

Things had started out all right the day before, when I'd arrived in this Central American country (let's call it Juanita). A delegation from the president met me at the airport and whisked me off in a fancy limo to the presidential palace, a couple of blocks from the place where I was going to be shot at within a day. There, in an ornate parlor on the second floor, I cooled my heels for only half an hour before the president himself invited me in for an audience.

He'd hired me to help him guarantee that the next election would be democratic. So it was in his best interests to keep me happy.

From the condition of the outside of the palace, I expected

him to mount a golden throne for his audience with me, but what I saw was a well-appointed office with a big desk, a computer, and a couple of armchairs. He motioned me into one of them and sat in the other. There was no one else in the room.

"It's good of you to come," he said in Spanish.

"Our company is very pleased that you engaged our services," I said in the same language.

"My servant has registered you at a good hotel only a few blocks away," he said. "Your luggage has been taken to your room."

"Thank you."

A knock at the door and someone brought in coffee on silver service. It was all terribly civilized, and that made me edgy.

"You understand," he said, looking suddenly presidential, "that I was elected democratically."

"Yes." Actually no, because anyone with smarts enough to work his way through a library could have known that the whole political world viewed his "election" as a monumental con job. But I wasn't ready to let on that I suspected him of anything but the best intentions.

"I have prepared a list"—he reached across to his desk and pulled off a file folder—"of people who would be willing to work with you to ensure that the coming electoral process is honest and fair."

"If you don't mind me asking, Mr. President," I said, "what assurances can you give me that the people on your list are independent of your influence? I'm sorry, but my employers require that I ask such questions."

He looked put out for a second, then said, "You will have to speak with those on my list. Each of them will be able to give you a statement regarding their freedom to speak and act."

"What would you like me to do?" I asked.

"Simply to advise those on the list about the proper procedures to follow in establishing an electoral process that will be both fair and seen to be fair. As you may know, there are some in the international community who have doubts about the honesty of our past elections. Thus I have arranged for a two-day seminar the day after tomorrow here at the palace for all who will be administering the election to come."

"To prepare myself," I said, "could you provide me with a car?"

He looked surprised. "If you need to travel, I will arrange for a car and driver. You will, of course, be free to go wherever you wish."

"I'd rather drive myself," I said.

"Where is it that you wish to travel?"

"Just here in the city. All I need is a vehicle and a map of the city."

"But I will provide one of my servants to guide you personally."

"That won't be necessary," I said, my words dragging a brief look of annoyance out of him before he agreed to my request. The last thing he wanted on my report to my boss was a statement that he'd been uncooperative.

So I was facing yet another put-up job and another country where democracy was only a word and the real democrats rotted in dungeons while the goons lived in palaces and sipped their coffee from silver service. I was fed up with it, especially with being the pawn in one more public relations scheme masterminded by one more corrupt president. My job was to consult with democratic movements and help them succeed, not to give my blessing to fake elections that would provide the monsters with a license to plunder the population for another five years.

The president's people rounded up a rental—an ancient Chevy sedan—and let me go, though the inevitable followers hovered close in two old Volvos. First stop was the main taxi stand at the center of town. Parking nearby, I put on my best saunter and started engaging the cabbies in conversation.

I was mostly interested in the list the president had handed me. Supposedly it named people of influence who were not under the thumb of the Juanitan government and who could engineer a fair election.

But the first driver I talked to collapsed into laughter when he read the list, then called his friends over to share the joke. I guess I shouldn't have told him that the names were honest men chosen by the president to produce a truly democratic vote.

When he'd calmed down a bit, my cabby explained. "These are the worst people in our country, señor," he said. "They ride in our taxis when they are not being driven in their luxury cars, and they speak openly about their riches and their corruption. These are the ones who pay for the secret police to make their enemies disappear."

"Who are their enemies?"

"Anyone who opposes them—lovers of freedom, those who resist their criminal commerce, the children in the streets who cause too much trouble with their begging. Such are the people who vanish and are never heard of again."

A small crowd of drivers had gathered. "Aren't you afraid to be speaking like this?" I asked him.

"We are taxi drivers. We are nothing. No one listens to us, señor."

So much for the list. It was everything I expected it to be—packed with members of the power elite who were all cronies of the president. If he was expecting a happy report out of me he was in for serious disappointment.

By late afternoon, I parked outside the president's palace, my Chevy polluting the whole block, and asked for another audience with his highness. He'd probably stayed informed of my movements, because the tails he sent out had been on me most of the time.

"I can't work with you," I told him. "The people on your list are too close to the center of power."

"Who did you expect me to find to organize the election?" he asked, his voice even, civilized, masking all evidence of frustration. "The peasants know nothing of such things."

"Every person on your list has a vested interest in seeing you returned to power."

"Then I will expand the list," he said.

"In what way?"

"There are others who could be included."

"More friends of yours?"

"You really are a very rude man," he said, tension breaking into his voice. "Please do not forget who is employing you."

"Mr. President," I said, "you haven't been dealing honestly with me. I have no choice but to discontinue our relationship."

"Please do not be so hasty, Mr. Sylvester," he said. "I feel certain that I can provide you with a better list by tomorrow."

"It would be good to be able to trust you to do that," I told him, rising. "But I simply can't believe you want a fair election here."

"What do you plan to do?" he asked.

"Write my report tonight, do some shopping for my children tomorrow, and leave on the noon plane."

"You can't be serious."

"Yes, I can." With that, I walked out on him. There isn't any reasoning with snakes when they have power. It was better to cut my losses than to have him go on toying with me.

That night I wrote much the same in my report, then phoned Karen to have her pick me up at the airport in Seattle. The next morning I fired up the Chevy to hunt down some souvenirs for the family, hoping to be back by ten-thirty, check out of the hotel, and take the twelve-thirty flight home. Of course, it didn't work out that way because someone blew my side mirror off and put a couple more bullets into the car, and now I was driving through the slums, wondering what to do.

After an hour of that, I decided to buy a ticket, and fly home. Libertec could reimburse me for my luggage.

I left the car in the parking lot in front of the terminal—someone else could retrieve it for the president. The thing was a piece of junk anyway. For a couple of minutes I scanned the front of the building—big, one-storied, stained white stucco, with dirty windows. There were only a few people going in or out, and I didn't at first see anyone who looked obviously like an undercover ghoul.

Which meant that secret police were probably all over the place, and I had no way of knowing what orders they'd been given about me. Reminding myself that I didn't have any other choice, I got out of the car and headed toward the front door of the airport building.

Twenty feet away from it, I realized that the reason why mousetraps are so dangerous is that they look like cheese boutiques.

CHAPTER TWO

He was on the phone. I remember a blue shirt and tense eyes that couldn't help flashing in my direction as I approached the front door of the airport. Whoever had organized the attack on my car near the president's palace probably hadn't expected me to make it as far as the terminal. This guy in the blue shirt was spooked at the sight of me.

I got to the door and even had it halfway open, then fingers grabbed at my sleeve and blue-shirt smashed his body into the door to block my way. I yanked my arm out of his clutches and ran, limping, down the front of the building, hearing him close behind me. I ran for the end of the building, hoping there was another door, because I believed they'd leave me alone once I was inside.

I rounded the corner and stopped dead. A man in a red checked shirt and jeans was standing in my way, his pistol held low—waist height. Behind me my blue-shirted pursuer came around the corner and barreled right into me, bashing me to the sidewalk.

I rolled on my back, panting, blood oozing from the heels of both of my hands. Blue-shirt was down too, but he got up faster than I did, one knee of his pants torn. The man in the red checks held his gun steady, pointed at my head. Carefully, hurting, I got to my feet.

They didn't say a word to me, just forced me between them in a bum's rush toward a taxi parked in the stand nearby. I could have shouted something, but these guys would probably just plug me where I was and run for it.

Blue-shirt and red-check crunched me into the back seat of the cab between them, and both of them bellowed at the driver to get going. Very slowly, the cabby eased the taxi out of the parking spot, then let it glide forward as if high speed was something he'd never heard of. He was smoking some sort of homemade cigar.

He turned his head to me, and said in Spanish, "Please buckle your seat belt, señor. The streets are dangerous."

Red-check thumped him on the arm with his pistol, then pointed the thing at his head. "Drive!" he shouted. "Drive very fast!"

The cabby gunned it down the street, shouting into the back seat, "You must buckle, señors. I am responsible for your safety." I decided to do what he said. The thugs on either side of me sneered and chose macho over wisdom.

So we shot down the congested street, my captors shouting directions as we went, the cab playing an endless game of chicken with everything in our way. City gradually turned to jungle interspersed with hayfields.

The car reeked of something the cabby must have picked up in a ditch and dried and rolled himself. He kept on smoking whatever it was heartily, despite the thugs and their gun. God, if I ever needed—

Then we swerved to avoid some junk on the road, wheels

sliding on the gravel shoulder, the driver correcting expertly, pulling us back on the pavement. He was going too fast for this potholed excuse for a highway.

Beside me blue-shirt squirmed, scared of the speed, but not wanting to slow our progress to wherever we were going. Red-check was leaning forward, his gun steady against the back of the cabby's head.

From my seat, I could see the speedometer creeping up to eighty, the road straight in front of us, a hayfield to the right, separated from the pavement by a ditch. Then the cabby whipped the steering wheel hard to the right, and we swerved off the road and hit the ditch and started to roll, instant disorientation, one flip, then two, bodies smashing into me on both sides, crashing sounds in my ears, then an end-for-end and we landed with a final thump, the car on its side, passenger side down.

Silence except for a hissing sound from somewhere. I couldn't see my captors. The cabdriver was still there in front of me, hung up sideways to the ground by his seat belt, not moving at first, then slowly straightening his head, looking forward, saying nothing.

I started exploring my body with my hands, searching for breaks, tears, wet spots. Everything seemed intact, and I could wiggle all my toes. Twisting myself so that my feet pointed down and my head up, I braced myself against the car door below me and unsnapped the seat belt. Then I was standing, crouched, my feet on one door and my head rammed against the other in the sideways-tilted cab.

I unlatched the door above me and pushed it upward. It groaned, hinges badly bent, and stayed open. Bracing against a front seat, I struggled up onto the side of the car, feeling it rock slightly. I crawled forward and pulled open the cabby's door.

"Hey," I shouted. He turned his head slowly and looked up

at me. "Are you hurt?" I asked him in Spanish.

Silence for a few seconds, then he said slowly, "I have no idea," so I checked him out as well as I could, and he seemed intact except for a cut on his forehead that was bleeding pretty badly.

"How many fingers?" I asked. He gave the right answer. "What day is this?" His response was dead on.

So I helped him up through the door, and we both slid to the ground and stared at the cab, still on its side. Totaled. One door was lying twenty feet away, right beside the body of blue-shirt. Red-check was ten feet the other way, a stone-cold crumpled ball. Both thrown clear.

The cabdriver sat down in the deep grass and put his face in his hands, blood from the cut on his forehead oozing through his fingers and staining his shirt. I tore off a good-sized chunk of my own shirt and used part of it to clean him up and part to tie around his head to stop the bleeding.

"I can't believe you did that," I said, starting to tremble, sitting down beside him.

"Knowing we were going to die made me reckless."

"The fuss you made about the seat belts—"

"They would not wear them if I demanded"—he took a deep breath—"demanded that they should."

"What's your name?"

"Fernando."

"Mine's Ben." We didn't bother shaking hands while we sat there in the deep grass. In fact, both of us were avoiding body movement as much as we could.

You had to give Fernando an A for sheer nerve. Crashing your car on purpose at eighty miles an hour takes a lot of it.

"We must make our escape," Fernando said.

"I thought we just did that."

"They will send others to look for us, just as my friends are even now searching for us in their taxis."

"Who is closer—friend or foe?"

"That is hard to say."

So we waited, somewhat sheltered by the deep grass, trying to watch the road through the blades weaving in the breeze. At least the car wasn't a flaming, smoking beacon, but it was clearly visible from the road and would have been even if we'd pushed it back onto its wheels.

Half an hour passed before I asked him, "Do you ever pray, Fernando?"

"Every Sunday in church and throughout this morning."

"I pray too."

Five minutes later a taxi went by, stopped, reversed, and a voice shouted in Spanish, "Fernando, where are you? It's Luis."

As fast as either of us could move, which would have made turtles sneer, we headed for the cab. The cane I usually relied on had been left behind outside the airport, so I limped awkwardly. Climbing inside the car, we followed Luis's instructions and scrunched ourselves down on the floor of the back seat.

Luis said nothing as we drove, and without being able to see anything out the windows, I had no idea where we were being taken, a fact that caused me to reflect again on how easy it was for me to fall into ridiculously dangerous situations. Being a political consultant, even one who helped emerging democratic movements, shouldn't have gotten me knifed one year, shot the next and now wrecked in a ditch. While the taxi slammed itself down the rough highway, I promised myself that I'd finally settle some things with Harry Simpson, my boss, if I survived the country of Juanita.

The taxi was going too fast for the road we were on, but I told myself to be grateful. The radio blessed us with music to a Latin beat.

An hour passed. Two. From the noises outside, we must have passed through three or four towns, the driver taking side routes, swerving a lot, braking, speeding up, punishing the car as he tried to cover more ground than seemed possible. Then suddenly we stopped in the middle of loud voices, all male, all talking at once.

"Come out of the car," our driver said.

I managed to get up on my knees, but I had to drag myself to my feet with the help of the seat-back ahead of me. Slowly I opened the taxi door and stepped down, propping myself with one hand. We were in a clearing in a jungle area, tents, men everywhere, some carrying aged rifles but wearing street clothes. If this wasn't a guerrilla enclave, it was a movie set.

Too many people were speaking too fast for me to follow much of the discussion. I guessed that the main issue was why I'd been brought to their secret hideaway which now wasn't secret anymore.

Five minutes of lively argument, and I could see that this was going nowhere, so I tapped the shoulder of the man who had driven us there—Luis—and shouted in his ear in Spanish, "Who's in charge? Take me to him."

No good. The boss was away, they told me. Finally they sat me down under a palm tree and told me not even to think of moving. Then, to influence my confidence, Luis drove off with Fernando. Neither of them had asked for payment despite the distance we had come.

I was so sick of this kind of thing happening that I almost wished Simpson would show up so I could throw my consulting job back in his face. But this time, at least, I wasn't nearly as afraid. Something happens to you when you're forced to grapple with your own mortality again and again. You learn to leave it to God, because you have no other real options open to you once you recognize how fragile you are

"Señor!" a voice shouted suddenly. I turned and saw a big man approaching me on foot. "You are quite a surprise," he said in English. He wore camouflage, and behind him was a dark green jeep that I hadn't heard pull up.

I said nothing.

"The president clearly has no love for you. Did you tell him that his now famous list was suspect?"

"Something like that," I said. "How did you—"

"The taxi drivers have certain sympathies with our cause." He sat down on the ground in front of me and hugged his knees. I took note of a broad, strangely flat face and a bushy mustache.

"What cause would that be?"

He only smiled and ignored the question. "We will put you across the border in a day or two."

"I have a family. They were expecting me on today's plane."

"We can't have everything, can we?" he said. "Even if communication with your family is impossible, you must be thankful that you still have your life."

"I'm thankful. You're really going to help me get out of the country?"

He smiled. "It's clear to me that you are my enemy's enemy, as they say. Don't worry. I will help you. But I would appreciate if you would tell me everything of your conversations with the president."

"I was hired as his consultant," I said. "Even if I didn't take the job, professional ethics would tell me that our conversations were privileged."

"Mr. Sylvester," he murmured, stretching out his legs as he sat there opposite me on the ground, "do you have any idea where you are?"

"Not really."

"Does anyone but us know exactly where you are?"

"No."

"Then let's discuss your conversations with the president. I'm afraid one of my failings is impatience."

I told him everything I could remember. Two days later, they put me into the next country along with my passport and traveler's checks. I had just enough money to buy a flight home.

What was really strange, though, was the fact that no one in that neighboring country questioned my being there, even though we hadn't crossed at a regular border post. Maybe it had something to do with the letter the guerrilla leader gave me to show every bureaucrat I met, a letter signed only "Hector."

CHAPTER THREE

I t was fascinating the way his fingers folded around the cigarette, claw-like, while it burned down to the filter. Harry Simpson. Chief of operations. He'd obviously forgotten how much the smoke irritated my lungs.

"Your last mission wasn't as satisfactory as OPSDEP had projected it to be," he said. Simpson always talked like that. OPSDEP was the Operations Department that made final decisions on virtually everything. Loosely translated, he was saying that Operations hadn't gotten the performance they wanted out of me. That, of course, made me the goat.

I watched across his oversized desk, failing as usual to read any message in his face. The man lived beyond the rest of us common folks in a bureaucracy that I found incomprehensible. OPSDEP knew how to link names with assignments and send people into tough situations. But I doubt that they understood the agents who actually did the work.

Since it didn't occur to me to be apologetic for blowing my last sortie, I told him what was on my mind: "I'm sick of being hung out to dry by you people. Doesn't anybody do any research around here? First there was that knife in the arm two years ago from a guy who had murder on his mind. Then that Africa fiasco—"

"I've told you," Simpson said. "We had intelligence from the highest level with that one. Every indicator told us that Saluso wanted a free election."

"And you landed me in the middle of an attempted coup."

"You would have read it the same way we did even if we'd given you all the data we had. The only reason we didn't tell you more was that we were operating by need-to-know."

"Need-to-know" was always a handy excuse. If anyone needed to know, it was me because I was the guy with bullets flying past his head. Nobody ever told me much of anything.

We sounded like a couple of CIA agents, for goodness sake, not employees of Libertec. Simpson had become such a master of bafflegab that you couldn't even hold a decent conversation with him anymore.

"And I suppose this latest thing was my fault," I said.

"We were worried that your injury had put you off your form. We gave you a simple scenario," he said. "Nothing covert. The president—"

"Dictator."

"The president wanted nothing more than advice. He wasn't looking for anything beyond some basic training sessions. We gave the mission to you because it seemed easy enough for—"

"What? A gimp? A has-been?"

He ignored the self-pity. I was embarrassed because I usually managed to beat it down before it burst into speech. The leg wasn't too bad. One shoe had to be built up. I'd bought a fancy cane that I'd lost in Juanita and had since replaced, and I had to take it easy or the leg would swell up. Not bad for a humble political advisor who didn't get into this game to play James Bond.

"They took a dislike to you. The president, all of his advisors."

"I never talked to any advisors, and the whole thing was a fake from the beginning," I told him. "They needed a stamp of approval from someone in the West so they could show that it was going to be a clean election."

"It was."

"You saw my report. The president was scamming us, stacking the committee with his own people, probably pulling dirty tricks on the other parties."

"I choose to interpret the circumstances more optimistically."

"People who have their heads in the clouds can't see where they're going."

"You're the one who abandoned the mission."

"Someone shot at me."

"Your side mirror broke. It could have been a rock."

"It wasn't a rock. And that wouldn't explain why I was grabbed by a couple of sleaze-balls and almost eliminated."

"No one said your assailants were under the orders of the president. So you got roughed up by a pair of thieves. Our operatives are trained not to whine, Ben."

"Meaning what?"

"Meaning that you're losing your touch. There was a time when we could send you out and you always got the job done. Now we're having second thoughts about sending you overseas again. Maybe you'd be better working for us at home."

I stared at him, a hard-looking man with a face like a granite tombstone, the only concession to his humanity being his thinning hairline. Ex-marine captain, seemingly devoted to duty, but I didn't trust him anymore, and I wasn't surprised to hear him planning to offer me a desk job. I'd rattled his cage once too often, and it was time for him to rein me in.

"Does anyone ever have second thoughts about you, Harry?" I asked softly.

"Why should they?"

"Because you seem pretty accident prone." He bristled at that. "In fact, Harry, something smells, and I'm surprised the folks in the tower aren't holding their noses."

Simpson blanched at that—Anger? Fear? We didn't normally talk about the tower, that realm further up the Libertec high-rise where the real bosses did whatever real bosses do. Simpson, chief of operations, was good enough for us little people.

"Are you making an accusation, Ben?" he asked, his voice masking whatever he felt.

"Why? Do you want something slanderous for the tape recorder in your desk?"

He squirmed slightly, then said, "I just want to understand what it is that's led you to believe that I harbor a desire to harm you."

"You know very well what it is."

Surprisingly, he smiled. "I'm sure your job has been tense recently, Ben," he said. "The world is getting more complicated all the time, and I don't blame you for taking on some elements of paranoia considering what you've been through. Actually, I have something completely different to offer you. Close to home, no risk. You might even get in some fishing."

"Fishing," I said.

"Like you and your dad must have done when you were younger."

"My dad didn't fish, and he died before I got out of my teens."

"We have someone coming in from Colombia," Simpson went on.

"A democratic country," I reminded him. "They don't need our kind of advising."

"He's okayed by their justice ministry," Simpson said, ignoring my objection. "Apparently there is some move among the coca growers to escape the tyranny of the cartels and get into a more legitimate form of agriculture. They need help organizing themselves."

"Since when did we become union organizers?"

He frowned. "Our client is going to meet you at a fishing resort on Harrison Lake."

"That's in Canada."

"It's all right. Canada immigration says you're all clear with them and can visit the country any time."

"Praise be," I said.

"We'd like you to meet him, do some fishing, talk. We're also considering setting up a more permanent base in Canada and having you head it up."

"A desk job?"

"I thought you were sick of high adventure."

There was no point in pursuing it. If they wanted to put me out to pasture, I'd have to weigh my options.

"So the coca growers have finally overcome their love for all the money they're making, not to mention their fear of the drug lords, and they've decided to organize."

"Our intelligence—" he began, but I was already getting out of the chair and heading for the door.

"There's a fifty-fifty chance, Harry," I said, "that I'll be clearing out my desk tomorrow. And if you use the word *intelligence* once more in my presence, I'll sneak into your house while you're sleeping and shave a happy-face on top of your head." Slamming his door with my foot as I went out was only icing on the cake.

I felt a pang about it, though, as I walked back to my office. Heaven wasn't nearly as pleased with my outburst as I'd been. And the conversation had taken me no closer to an explanation of why every mission I took went sour on me. It had to be Simpson. Either he'd become incompetent or he actually wanted me to fear for my life every time I left the country.

I packed up early and started the long journey home to Lynden while the sun was still high. Home to Karen. I wondered what mood she'd be in. After I'd flown in from Central America two days before, she'd been crying all over the phone during my call from the SeaTac airport, and she'd greeted me on our front step with a hug that sucked the life out of me. Even the kids were more reserved.

Later that night she'd come into the living room where I was sprawled, resting, and I'd seen the determination on her face.

"You have to quit," she said.

"This job is what I do," I answered.

"Only until you're dead, Ben."

"I've got a lot more going for me than I used to."

"Who? God? He's the one who keeps letting you fall into trouble. Where was he when our helicopter was being shot out of the sky? Where was he when Saluso shot you?"

"We survived against amazing odds. Stop blaming God."

She sat on the floor in front of me. "Then you tell me what's happening, Ben," she said. "You're getting calmer and calmer about everything, and I'm falling to pieces."

"You could go to a counselor."

"How's that going to help us?" She gave me a searching look. "Why do you insist on simplifying this?"

"Because I'm a simple guy," I said, "and I expected a better welcome back than I'm getting."

"You almost died!" she shouted back.

So had gone my first evening since the Juanita disaster, and another day off didn't improve things much. As I got off I-5 at Bellingham and headed north on Meridian Drive, I realized I wasn't too keen about going home to more outbursts or the cold silence that inevitably followed.

Jimmie was in the front yard playing with his parachuting soldier. No doubt Jack would be inside reading. At nine years old, Jack was decades older than his eight-year-old brother, and it worried me.

"Look at this thing fly, Dad," Jimmie shouted.

"It's great," I told him, heading for the front door.

"Can you come out and play? Kyle's got the flu."

"Maybe in a while, Jimmie. Where's Mom?"

"Doing laundry."

I found her in the middle of transferring a load from the washer to the dryer. She looked exhausted, so I took the load from her.

She stared at me for a few seconds and then she said, "I'm sorry."

"No need to be."

"Yes there is. When you weren't at the airport, I went crazy. I called Harry Simpson, and he had no idea what had happened to you. I thought Libertec usually sent people along to watch over their consultants if there was any danger."

"Simpson thought it would be a piece of cake."

She brushed away some hair that had fallen over one side of her face. "I don't want to be angry at you, Ben. You don't have to quit. It's..." She paused, tears showing.

I held her. "Simpson says they might have a posting for me closer to home. In Canada. He wants me to go up in a couple of weeks for a short trip, but they may be setting up a permanent base there."

"Would you be happy?" she asked.

"I'm sick of getting shafted every time I fly out of here. Maybe it's time for something more stable. How would you feel about living in Canada?"

"You'd be safe?"

"Yes." It was a moment of profound understanding. We both knew that the days of Ben Sylvester, international adventurer, had to end sometime.

I coaxed Jack out of his room and took him and Jimmie to the park to play catch. Good old domesticated Ben.

CHAPTER FOUR

Coming out of the McDonald's at Squamish, we took the Sea to Sky Highway in the direction of Whistler Village, marveling still at the unexpected vacation and the fabulous scenery. It was all a gift from Simpson—surprise. My boss owned a time share in a condo at the famous resort north of Vancouver, Canada, and had phoned me at home to offer it to us for a week. Free.

Not that I was fooled. Harry Simpson, even in his best moments, was a devious man, and it was plain to me that this was his way of asking me to lay off on my half-formed accusations against him. From my point of view, though, the week would give me more time to figure out why he always seemed ready to send me to my death.

"I see a bear!" Jimmie shouted from the back seat, pointing up a slope.

"Tree stump," Jack said. "Not a bear."

"It's a bear. Really, Daddy. Right there. A big one."

I let them argue it out after Karen and I had shared a grin. Those two never agreed on anything, and competition was fierce between the young fry of the Sylvester household.

The road continued winding precariously, the narrowness of it giving few chances to pass slow-moving campers and trailers. For a place that was the number-one ski resort in North America in the winter, it was a rugged climb to reach it even in the middle of summer. Still, I looked forward to the break before I took Simpson's little job at Harrison Lake and met the representative of the mythical ex-coca growers of Colombia.

"You're very quiet today," Karen said.

"Lost in the scenery," I said.

"You're thinking about Harry, aren't you? You sure he's the one responsible for what's happened to us?"

"I don't know," I said. "Suppose for a minute that you're a little errand girl, and the first place you're sent, you get beaten up. Just a fluke, right? So you go on to your second job and someone throws a rock at you. Maybe just another fluke, but eventually you're going to wise up. Who was it, Goldfinger, that said, 'Once is happenstance, twice is coincidence, but three times is enemy action'?"

"You've had your third time," she said.

"But I still can't figure out the motive. He's never liked me much, but firing me would be a whole lot easier than having me killed on the job."

"Let it rest for a while, Ben," she said. "We're supposed to be enjoying ourselves."

I wasn't sure what that meant. For the past six months, I'd been a complete dud while I rebuilt the strength I'd lost after getting shot in the leg. I'd probably been miserable to have around the house. Karen was dealing with anger, Jack with depression. Jimmie, our youngest, was the only person left with enough zest to carry him happily through the average day. A regular soap opera family, we were.

"A bear!" Jimmie shouted again.

"Is not," Jack said automatically, but this time it was—a small black crossing a meadow further up the ridge to the right of us. We slowed to watch it, cemented together for the moment in shared wonder.

None of us had ever been to Whistler Village, and it turned out to be an experience. A tightly woven, totally planned community, it sported monster hotels and dozens of small shops. Summer had brought out the bicyclers and in-line skaters to challenge the drivers for pavement space. Fanning out from the town core were Whistler and Blackcombe Mountains, both enormous and both served by gondolas and chairlifts that even in midsummer were in constant use.

The place was a fantasy world for the rich or the spendthrift. Our condo alone, when we finally found it in the maze of the village's convoluted streets, would have cost us over three hundred a night if we'd been paying for it. Thank you, Harry Simpson.

We got ourselves settled, the kids choosing a hide-a-bed in the loft. Karen wandered off to buy groceries in the village while I explained to Jack and Jimmie the operations and rules of the hot-tub. North American decadence at its very best.

I found myself reveling in the grand illusion that this was life as it should be—no treacherous enemies, no devious clients, no Simpson. An oasis in the midst of the angst of living.

The next morning, it was up the two-stage chairlift to a spot near the top of Blackcombe Mountain, where we watched skiers and snowboarders still racing down the glacier even in the midst of summer. The view of the valley floor—village, lakes, golf courses, forest—was fabulous, and the kids were suitably terrified by the chairlift as they dangled forty feet off the steep slope on the way down.

That's what I treasure—the beginning of that week in the

false world of Whistler—because it shone so brightly in contrast to the darkness that hovered just beyond our vision while we frolicked in the pleasure of the place.

We'd arrived on a Monday, and early Tuesday evening, wanting to check out a bookstore in the village, I left Karen and the kids in the condo with a video and set out for some exploring on my own. I remember that the air was cool enough for a sweater and that the peace I felt as I wandered the pedestrian-only town center was palpable.

I was as contented as a sacrificial lamb on the eve of Passover, pampered, cleaned-up, secure, unknowing.

The bookstore was near the place where Karen had bought our groceries, and I was surprised to see how well-stocked it was. Obviously, not everyone who came to Whistler in the summer was into long hikes or gondola rides. Craving escapism, I chose the latest John Grisham and started back toward the condo.

"Ben." The voice came from behind me just as a hand touched my shoulder, and I whirled, startled, ready to defend myself. And then I stared, frozen to the ground, the book dropping from my hand, my knees starting to rubberize as I stopped breathing. There was a bench nearby, and I groped for it, sat down, still not breathing.

"Are you all right?" He ran to a sidewalk cafe nearby and came back with a paper cup full of water and handed it to me. I drank the water down, then went into a fit of coughing.

Through blurred vision I stared at him, trying to confirm to my mind that he was no illusion, that the man standing in front of me was indeed Jeff Mancuso.

"Where," I said, my voice rasping with the after-effects of the coughing. "Where have you—" I choked, cleared my throat, wiped my eyes.

Two years. Almost two years of not knowing. My wife Karen had been kidnapped by some utterly evil people who drugged her out of her mind. And Jeff. Unexplainable Jeff. He was there with me when I went after Karen and found her, and in the process I killed him, burned him to death in a fire that I started deliberately. But no one found his body and—

"Can I get you anything?" he asked, sitting on the bench next to me.

"Coffee," I said, when I stopped coughing. "You've got things to tell me. Over there."

We walked to the outside cafe, ordered coffees. Jeff sat opposite me, but we were suddenly awkward, neither of us knowing how to start.

I finally spoke. "When you didn't come out of the flames, and I couldn't reach you..." I stopped, blinking. "We had to leave. To rescue our kids. We had to get away."

"It's all right," he said.

"My fault. The fire—I killed you."

He smiled. "You tried but you failed. I'll always be faster and smarter than you."

"I didn't want anybody to get hurt. Especially not you or Karen."

"Is Karen okay?"

"Fine. She's fine."

"I know. I'm not sure why I asked."

"What do you know, Jeff?" I asked him. "How did you get here? Where have you been for that matter? We went out of our minds. Your brother too."

"Sorry," he said. "They didn't want you to know in case you put the operation in danger. I really tried, Ben, but they insisted."

I stared at him as he picked up his coffee and gulped it,

wincing at the heat. He must have known I didn't have a clue what he was talking about, but he didn't elaborate.

"Jeff," I said.

"What?"

"You're supposed to tell me where you've been."

"They actually want you to know now," he said. "That's why I followed you up here. This place is out of the way."

"Who?"

"Who what?"

"Are you messed up in some kind of cult?" I asked. "You're not making any sense." He looked the same for the most part—rugged square jaw, tough lean build, curly hair. But I could see signs of scarring on his face, and his skin was too smooth to be natural.

"Where do you want to start?"

"At the fire," I said. "We thought you were dead. Something fell out of the ceiling and buried you."

"Maybe that's what it looked like from your side, but I only caught a piece of it. Knocked me down, but I crawled into the kitchen where most everything had already burned. Phil never had a chance."

"Never deserved one," I said. "I didn't see you. I thought you'd been crushed along with Phil."

"Even when I got to the kitchen it was too hot, so I ran out the back door so I could breathe. Apparently I was pretty burned."

"Apparently?"

"Total blank after that. The next thing I knew, I was waking up in a hospital bed in Calgary."

"Five hundred miles from Kelowna? How'd you manage that?"

"Search me. I was in a special ward with a cop outside the door."

"And?"

"Skin grafts. I was in there a couple of months."

"Who paid for it?"

"They did."

"Jeff." I looked into his face and saw a familiar dance, the pupils of his eyes flitting as he tried to pirouette among my questions without falling over or having his costume come off. "Who is they?" I asked.

He sighed and ran his fingers through his hair. "CSIS," he said, pronouncing it like a word—*seesis*.

"Who?"

"Canadian Security Intelligence Service. Sort of like the CIA and the FBI combined. You see..." He paused, trying to read my reaction. "You and I uncovered spies in your father-in-law's electronics company. When the police found Phil dead in the fire and heard about the secrets being sold to the Middle East, they called in CSIS."

"Someone must have found you wandering around in the snow, burned and incoherent. CSIS connected you with the fire and moved you to Calgary?"

"At first they just wanted information. Then they asked me if I'd work with them undercover."

"Sure they did. With what training?"

"They've got a nasty reputation for using all kinds of people, trained or not. When I was released from the hospital, I got a job assembling electronics equipment back in Electar."

The image flashed at me for a second—Okanagan Valley, near Kelowna, British Columbia. The town where I started the fire.

"And you didn't contact anybody you knew to tell the world you're alive?"

"My brother Dave. I swore him to silence."

"My mother-in-law runs the company. Surely she must have known."

"She never comes to Electar, and I used a different name."

"Why not me? A simple phone call, collect even. Thirty seconds to say you were fine."

"They said it was because of your mother-in-law. She doesn't know there are still spies trying to sell secrets to the Middle East and not succeeding much except for disinformation."

"And you were afraid I might let something slip to her?"

"That was part of it."

"What's the rest? Come on, Jeff." I pushed my coffee cup away, leaned back and stared at him.

"It's only just now that I got authorization to tell you this. Remember when you got stabbed in South America, just before you met me? You found out that someone in your company told the wrong people where you were, and that's why you took a knife in the arm."

"Tell me what I don't know."

"There's a connection between the spy network and Libertec. A big connection." Jeff hadn't lost his flare for the dramatic.

"Who's the link?" I asked.

"I was working in Electar, keeping my nose clean except when I was snooping for CSIS. We know the identity of the spy there, and I'd been watching who he contacted. Then one day about a month ago, someone from your company met this guy I was watching. They tried to keep it secret, but I spotted them and got a couple of photos. The visitor was—"

"Let me guess," I said. "Harry Simpson."

"Yeah."

"So what's the connection?"

"We don't know yet, but we want you in on the basic facts."

"So I can go to work on the side for a Canadian spy agency? No thanks."

"They're very good," he said. "We're offering you a chance to get the man responsible for all the trouble you've been having. At least we think he's responsible. If he checks out, you can watch him go down."

"I thought you were big into Christian charity, Jeff, not revenge."

"Justice. That's what everyone wants. I thought you might be delighted in the fall of the wicked so you could gloat. I seem to remember you liked to gloat."

"Not anymore. I'm into Christian charity myself now."

"You?"

"Me."

"Will you help us?"

I got up from the table and tossed down one of those amazing Canadian two dollar coins. "Maybe. What do you want exactly?"

"Harry Simpson asked you to do a job at Harrison Lake. Take it as you planned, but go armed and be very careful. You can't take a gun into Canada, but we'll leave one for you." He told me where. "Be very careful."

"Of what? If you're setting me up for another mess, Jeff, so help me—"

"I'll be there. I'll back you up." He gave me that familiar look of intense honesty, and I felt a chill because this guy was a master of surprises. What was more, CSIS knew more than Jeff had told me if they'd actually gotten wind of the assignment Harry had given me at Harrison Lake.

"Come back to our condo and say hello to Karen and the kids," I offered.

"No thanks. Gotta go." He left a couple of bucks on the table and walked away. As I watched him disappear around a corner, I wondered if he'd been one of those apparitions, like a little space-man who takes you to see the wonders of the universe, then leaves you bewildered on your front lawn.

CHAPTER FIVE

H e told me his name was Pancho, not that it mattered, and that he'd flown into Vancouver from Colombia the day before as representative of the repentant coca growers of South America, or whatever name he'd devised for them. No one had followed him to Harrison, he was certain.

It was a fabulous day, and the little town of Harrison was everything a Canadian resort on the edge of a large mountain lake should be and then some. Lots of hotels and restaurants, but everything low-key in the Canadian way. The lake was to the north, big, surrounded by tall rounded evergreen-covered mountains.

I'd driven up from Lynden, Washington, through Abbotsford, then across the Fraser River to Mission and east to Harrison. Vancouver was only a couple of hours west, but my surroundings made me believe that I'd found the true Canadian wilderness.

We met at a lodge up the eastern side of the lake. Pancho and I casually greeted one another at the dock, striking up a conversation when he learned that I spoke Spanish, deciding to throw in our lot together for a day of fishing, splitting the cost of a twelve-foot rented boat, as if none of this had been carefully prearranged.

Pancho was a big man, so I made him sit in the middle while I took a steering position in the stern. When we set out, he grinned with pleasure, like a kid on his first carousel ride. I remembered the thirty-eight in my fishing box, under a false cover in the bottom, because I was scared of this guy from the second I saw him. Presumably Jeff and his people were somewhere around, but my client and I soon left a lot of open water behind us as we trolled across the lake.

Then, ten minutes out, just as my heart rate was starting to slow down to normal, Pancho motioned for me to shut down the motor.

"May I request, Mr. Sylvester," he said in Spanish, "that you remove your shirt?"

"Why?"

"We must be sure that nothing is recorded." I took off my shirt and tossed it to him. "Now the trousers."

I gave him a look but did what he wanted. A few seconds later, after rumpling through my clothes, he threw them back.

"I am terribly sorry," he said, "but many lives may be put at risk by a little carelessness."

"That's all right," I said, surprising myself at how well I hid my irritation.

"Go to that island, please," he said, pointing at Echo Island, an enormous chunk of tree-covered earth that rose almost vertically out of the lake to a tall rounded peak.

I started the motor, heading for the north side, noticing as I did so that there were very few boats on the lake. The nearest one was a canoe with one occupant. He'd paddled all the way from the town of Harrison and looked like he meant to pass west of

Echo Island as I began searching for a landfall on the north end.

The shoreline was so steep that I'd almost given up trying to land when I spotted an indentation wide enough to take a couple of boats. Above it, the slope was far from level, but I figured we could find a spot to sit and talk if that's what he wanted.

"Is this all right?" I asked Pancho, and he gave me an obliging shrug.

He leaped out of the boat as we reached shore, tied it quickly to a rock, and motioned for me to join him in a scramble up the slope. He carried his small pack of fishing gear, so I picked up my tackle box, knowing full well that fishing wasn't on either of our minds.

We found a spot that was almost level, trees surrounding a bare patch about six feet across. Pancho sat down with his back against a trunk and motioned me to sit opposite him. By now I was watching every movement he made, hoping that I'd spot anything sinister before it fell on me. Jeff had promised backup, but I saw no sign of it or of him.

Pancho smiled to put me at ease. "Thank you for your patience with me," he began. "This place is not my home, and I worry about my enemies." From the size of him, it was his enemies who should have been worrying.

"It's peaceful here," I said, casually opening the tackle box and fiddling with a few weights. "Why don't you explain to me what's happening among your people."

"Of course. As you know, the coca has been very good for farmers in my country. We have a better standard of living now though once we might have starved."

"But the government and the police have mounted stiff opposition," I said. "Important cartel leaders have been arrested."

"Yes." He leaned forward. "That is why a large number of us

have decided that financial security is not necessarily the highest good. We want to organize ourselves, cooperate with the government and negotiate a way to begin a new method of agriculture."

Above, high on the slope, a branch cracked, and I thought of all the bear stories I had heard. But no other sound followed except the drone of a high-powered boat, far away but approaching, presumably headed past the island toward the north end of the lake. Everything was so idyllic that I had trouble connecting Pancho with the lies he was telling me.

"Why don't we leave that story behind," I said, "and turn to the real reason why we're here."

He looked concerned, but not overly so. "I don't understand your question, Mr. Sylvester," he said.

"Call me Ben," I told him, fingering the catch to the secret compartment at the bottom of my tackle box. "We both know that the coca growers aren't organizing against the cartels. The money's too good and the risks are too high."

"Let me show you something," he said, reaching for his pack and opening it. I flipped the catch inside my tackle box, but he didn't seem to notice. The gun was in my hand now, still hidden in the box.

He fumbled with his pack for a few seconds, then with a sudden flourish he whipped out a pistol of his own and turned it on the slope above us, not on me. And my gun was out now, pointed at Pancho's head, but he was ignoring me, looking up the slope as the sound of the approaching boat grew louder.

"Show yourself!" he shouted in Spanish. "I see you and I am well armed." For a few seconds there was silence, then a rustling about a hundred feet above us, and someone appeared from behind a tree and began moving down the hill.

"Pancho!" I shouted.

"What?" He turned his head and saw my gun.

"Drop it."

"Would you like me to shoot this man?" he asked, looking up the slope as the person coming down moved closer and transformed himself into the familiar gait of my old friend, Jeff Mancuso.

Thank you so very much, Jeff. Thank you from the bottom of my heart, and I laid the gun down on the ground where neither Pancho nor I could reach it easily. Jeff stumbled down the last few yards, his three left feet almost dumping him on his face, and then he was there, standing in front of Pancho, his back to me.

"Take off your clothing," Pancho said in Spanish.

"What?" Jeff asked.

"Strip," I told him in English. "He wants to see if you're armed." The noise of the approaching boat was louder still.

"I'm not armed," he said, keeping his back to me.

"Show him," I said. Jeff obliged, skinning down to his underwear. He was packing nothing of any danger to Pancho except for a Swiss army knife that Pancho put in his pocket.

"Dress yourself and sit beside Mr. Sylvester," Pancho said. Jeff did what he was told and the two of us sat side by side.

"Where are the rest of your men?" I asked Jeff quietly, watching the big boat I'd been hearing come around the point and aim itself right at us. Thirty-footer, powerful motor, built for speed rather than stability. Probably launched at the public ramp in Harrison. I was under no illusion that it was there by chance or that it was loaded with police. The look of rapture on Pancho's face as it approached told me what I needed to know.

"Where's your backup?" I repeated to Jeff, who hadn't said a word since he'd re-buttoned his shirt.

"They had somebody at the lodge," he told me, looking warily at Pancho who seemed to have no grasp of English. "The guy phoned me when you arrived, and I took a canoe out. When I saw you land here, I beached it a couple of hundred yards away and came overland."

"A canoe? You came unarmed in a canoe to back me up?"

"I like canoes."

"Is a rescue in the offing?" I asked Jeff as Pancho got up and waved to the crew in the boat.

"The guys at the lodge went to a meeting. They didn't think this Pancho fellow would be much of a risk so soon after he'd arrived. I was supposed to get close, do some listening, and report back." Jeff flashed me his now familiar guilty look.

"Don't you recognize turkey soup when you're floating in it?" I asked him.

His expression was pained. "We could pray, you know," he said. I gave him a look.

The approaching boat was manned by two tough-looking guys who had no obvious weapons but gave the impression that they needed no more than their bare hands to be effective. They pulled back the throttle and let the boat drift in bow first until it barely touched the shore right beside our rented fishing boat. One of the men jumped out and tied a rope to an outcropping of rock.

Conference time. The men started talking with Pancho, quietly so as not to disturb the prisoners, but I heard words like "two of them" and "more money" all in Spanish, and it became clear that our new visitors were hired guns who weren't too happy to have Jeff as an extra victim unless they got more of a payoff. I looked at Jeff to see what he was understanding, but his face reflected only bewildered shock.

After a few minutes, Pancho gave up the argument and handed the two thugs a wad of U.S. dollars out of his wallet. Grins all around except for Jeff and me, who had somehow lost the party spirit.

"Let's go," said one of the goons, speaking in English now.

"Where?" Jeff asked.

"What's it to you? Move." The guy pulled his own pistol in imitation of Pancho. So it was down the slope for us and into the big powerboat. Why fight the inevitable?

The boat was built on low sleek lines, no cabin cruiser. Ten seats, long pointy bow, throbbing engine that opened to a scream when we cast off and they cranked it up. Jeff and I sat beside each other near the stern, with Pancho using his gun to hold us at bay.

If it hadn't been for the circumstances and the company we were keeping, the ride north across open water would have been quite a thrill. The sun was blazing, the water was rippling, the evergreen forests covering the mountains on all sides of us were doing their very best to shout the glory of God. Once we'd passed a long low island we even had a view ahead of us of a snow peak.

But my mind was working too hard on the problem at hand to let me reflect long on the beauties of nature. Clearly this snatch had been planned. Pancho hadn't signaled anyone, yet these guys had shown up as if they had a prior invitation. People are kidnapped because they're valuable to someone. What value did I have that would justify this kind of planning? Jeff was just along for the ride, but these guys had gone to a lot of trouble and expense to get their hands on me. Why?

I told myself that Simpson was done for if I ever got my hands on him. Any doubts I'd ever had about who was behind all the foul-ups I'd endured were now gone. It was Simpson. Jeff had told me as much, and Simpson was the one who had urged me to meet Pancho at Harrison Lake.

We'd been racing north for half an hour, the heavy motor loud in our ears, when I saw a seaplane coming in low over the western mountains—a two-engine, white with blue trim. With no wasted motion, it landed ahead of us about half a mile away. I looked at Jeff, but before I could utter a question, the man driving our boat answered it for me by turning and heading straight for the plane.

What in the world? This had turned into a major operation with me at the center of it. How could I be worth that much to anyone? Libertec had a very strict and very public "no ransom" policy. These guys must have known—

"Ben," Jeff said to me over the sound of the motor.

"What?"

"Let's talk to them. If they knew my connections—"

"Shut up," I said. "You tell them about your connections, and you're a dead man. They didn't organize this little show for your benefit, and it won't take much provocation for them to dump your body over the side."

"Silence," Pancho shouted in Spanish. The two men were keeping their distance from us, one driving the boat and the other a good ten feet away, a gun pointed at us every second.

We were much closer to the plane now, a large impressive-looking thing, propellers still spinning, and I wondered whether maybe we should have just pitched ourselves overboard and swum for it.

We pulled alongside and they bundled us into the plane and made us belt up tight. Then the copilot or whatever he was, a small guy with a macho mustache, came over, a little box in his hand. He pulled out a syringe, loaded it from a bottle and plunged it into my upper arm right through my shirt. Turning to

Jeff, he reloaded the same syringe and stuck it into my buddy as well.

When my mind started to drift, I remember thinking that the whole thing had been pretty unsanitary and I didn't want strange germs in me.

That wouldn't be safe.

CHAPTER SIX

I t was a very dark night, and we were lost, Karen and I, and she said, "You were supposed to be my strength, Ben," and I said to her, "I thought you were free of that. No one can protect you from everything."

I was angry that she couldn't understand that life takes pokes at all of us, that we live in a fallen world and God never ever said we were immune. But my anger did nothing to overturn the reality that we were lost and struggling through some kind of fog. At first I thought that I was driving the car, but when I looked closer it became clear that we were walking together on a dark and lonely road.

Tipping suddenly, feeling something tight against my chest and stomach, Karen falling away from me, screaming, "Ben!" disappearing into the maw of the fog, her shout fading, and I was terribly afraid because I could do nothing for her.

Hard impact, bouncing, jostling, then silence until someone dragged me backwards, heels bumping. I tried to get upright and walk, but my legs had given out and Karen was nowhere to be seen or heard. Rocking gently on something for the longest time, then something very tight around my chest, under my arms, pulling me, pulling me up into the darkness, so black.

Black like the darkness of that first month in the hospital in Bellingham after they shipped me home from Africa, after Songo Saluso put a bullet in my leg. And I was surprised that the memory was so vivid of those days when I finished the wrestling match and God finally pinned me, one, two, three, rising up off the mat so that he could stare at my fallen, broken form.

I didn't have to fight him, of course. It was stupid to fight him, but then I'd always been a stupid man, too dense to understand what was good for me. So when I saw him standing over me beside the mat, so to speak, I told him that I was too tired to wrestle anymore.

I told him the same through that whole dark month in the hospital in Bellingham while Karen came every day and even the kids were let in once in a while. I told him that I'd never go another round with him, but still the darkness went on, even with my family around me. Until one day it lifted and I felt my life seeping back into my bones, like a flame that didn't burn, only warmed. And I heard him say, "You are mine," and the thought of it gave me no fear at all.

A cot, narrow, hard. Rough blanket. Rocking, everything pitching as if I were riding out a slow-moving earthquake. I looked beside me and saw Jeff sleeping a few feet away on his own cot. Jeff, I thought you were dead. Then I remembered that he'd spoken to me somewhere. Whistler. Island. Drifting.

You see, I used to be the strong one, and Karen clung to me, afraid of her shadow and everyone else's. Then one day she met Jesus and he transformed her, and I couldn't get past it until I met him too. But she'd never wrestled with him—it's not ladylike—she'd never fought him and discovered—

Discovered what? That he was stronger? Of course he's

stronger, any fool knows that. No, discovered that he loved her more than she could love him.

Love him, Karen. Love him. Don't glare like that, don't tell him the should haves, as if he needed the lecture to expand his horizons.

Voices. Intrusions into a mind so confused, and I struggled as if I were swimming up from the bottom of a well, struggled through the murk to hear the voices because I sensed how important it was to know what they were saying.

Surfaced. Blinking. A cot. Everything moving. Jeff Mancuso still sleeping across a narrow aisle, and the voices clear now, speaking Spanish.

"The body has limits," the one said.

"Explain them," the other said.

"One more, who knows? They could die."

"Or not?"

"I can't be sure. Do they need another dose?"

"You said they'd be awake within the hour."

"Hector won't like the risk."

The voices disappeared. Where were we? Obviously from the metal room and the rolling motion, on a ship. How long since we'd left Harrison Lake? Unknown. My watch had a date function but someone had stripped me of everything—clothes, watch, wedding ring.

"Jeff," I whispered. Nothing. "Jeff." Louder. I reached over and tweaked his nose, and he made a face, his eyes still shut tight. At least he was alive.

Noises out in the hallway. Footsteps on metal, a key turning, and I squinted at the light coming in from the outside, far brighter than the dim night-light they'd left on in our room. Only one of them standing there. I could have jumped him if all my muscles had been ready to jump with me. He held a syringe, of course.

"No," I said, feeling very weak, "not again," like a grim torture scene in a bad movie. But he plunged it into me and suddenly I was having a conversation with God.

"This is not the end yet, Ben," he said.

"Even if I live, will it make any difference? I'm very tired. Karen is angry at you. Jack's messed up, my son..."

"Karen needs time," he said. "She just needs some space," and I knew I was only talking to myself. I was drifting again, and I saw her coming toward me. I knew she was going to say that she'd begged me to quit and now it was too late.

She'd begged me not to start the fire, and Jeff Mancuso, my good friend, burned up in it. But Jeff was alive, and I was not guilty, as free as the air. Then why was there so much weight on me, so much baggage?

I was rational now, watching Karen approach out of the mist. She was smiling, seemingly full of God's love once again. Then I looked closer and she was frightened, looked closer and she was angry, closer and she was weeping and the word coming out of her mouth again and again was "Ben."

Dark, and I was awake. The bulb in the night-light must have gone out. "Jeff," I said.

"Yeah." His voice told me that he was very close.

"Are you all right?"

"I've been awake a couple of hours, I think. You were talking a lot and I'm wondering if they scrambled your brain."

"Thanks. What did I say?"

"That you killed Jeff and you're not really a good man and Karen must be healed. Simple stuff."

"Actually, I didn't kill you."

"No kidding."

"We're on a ship," I said, realizing that he probably already knew that.

"So?"

"So where are your people?"

"Nowhere. They're not coming after us." It would have been great to see his face, to see how hard he was struggling with his guilt and dismay.

"You dropped the ball this time, Jeff," I said. Silence. "Earth to Jeff," I said. "Hello." Silence.

"Come on, Ben. I messed up royally, all right, but now we've got to pull together or we'll never get out of here. They're probably going to kill us as soon as they think we've served our purpose."

"Which is?"

"How should I know? Look, your Harry Simpson was running guns to rebels in a certain Central American country."

"He's not my Harry Simpson, and what was the name of the country?" I said, getting that pain in my gut that happens every time I know the answer to a question before I ask it.

"Juanita." He didn't say "Juanita", but that's my name for the place.

"I met some of those rebels," I said. "They helped me escape. So what does Harry Simpson's nasty little scheme have to do with this luxury cruise we're on?"

"Your contact at Harrison Lake—this Pancho—he had a Colombian passport, but he flew to Canada from Juanita."

"You knew that?"

"Only on the morning you met him."

"So he probably wasn't the spokesman for the repentant coca growers of Colombia after all," I said. "So much for my faith in human nature."

I turned to lie on my back and stare at the ceiling above me, invisible in the darkness. Think, Ben. Figure it out. But there was only a blank where the answers should have been. And right in the middle of the blank was a spot reserved for Jeff and me.

Without warning, a key sounded in the lock and the door swung open. It was only a thug with food. He thumped the wall, and our dim night-light came on, flickering at first and then growing as steady as half a watt could be.

The food was simple—tortillas, some kind of bean dish in tomato sauce—but we needed strength and nourishment so both of us dug in while our waiter sneered at us from the doorway. When we'd finished, he took the plates and forks away without ever saying a word.

"Ben?" Jeff said after a few minutes, and I recognized that he was starting into his hesitant suggestion routine.

"Yes?"

"We're on a ship, right? How about trying a diversion? If one of us can escape this room, there's bound to be a two-way radio on board."

"If one of us can escape, it will take a miracle." I closed my eyes. "Let me think."

"You meant it earlier about your faith?" he asked. I could sense him staring at me, but I didn't want to open my eyes. "You're a believer?"

"What it is," I said, "is that I gave up trying to fight God. He's too strong once he gets hold of you."

"That's it? Your whole faith is that you gave up your fight with him?"

"No. He's turned everything around for me. But it's hard, you know, to talk—"

"No more than it is for me, Ben." His voice was too eager,

and it made my stomach squirm. "But he's real, isn't he? He's alive."

"I know."

"We have to talk to him about this."

"I have been."

"No, I mean together. Where two or three are gathered."

"OK, together."

We prayed until the dim bulb in our room started to flicker again, and I banged the wall to get it going. Then someone shouted, "Silence!" from outside the door so we moved down to whispers, batting around ideas, suggestions, anything that might get us out of this mess.

But nothing felt remotely like a solution. When you're locked into the bowels of an unknown ship sailing on an unknown ocean, there are just too many barriers to planning an escape. We soon gave up on the idea of jumping a guard and fleeing the room we were locked into.

I was bothered by something I remembered in the conversation I'd overheard between the two guards outside in the hallway. One of them had said something like "Hector won't like the risk." I wasn't sure how common the name Hector was, but I had a feeling he was referring to someone I'd already met.

Put it together, Ben. If Harry Simpson is selling guns to the rebels in Juanita, then those very same rebels captured you and Jeff, and this ship is rebel controlled.

They carefully planned their capture of you, and it didn't have anything obvious to do with Jeff and his contacts in the Canadian spy agency.

They wanted you, Ben. Why? What possible good could you be to them? They already had you once. Why didn't they hold onto you if they needed you so badly?

That was the biggest puzzler. I wasn't worth anything to anyone in Juanita. I didn't hold any enormous secrets, nor did I have an ounce of power to do anything for either side in the coming conflict between the president's people and the Juanitan rebels. The only answer that made even a glimmer of sense was that Simpson had paid them extra to get rid of me. But why not just bump me off—Jeff too for that matter—on Echo Island in Harrison Lake?

We had virtually nothing to help us understand this. Whatever our destination, we probably weren't coming back alive.

For about four more days, the ship sailed on while we were graciously allowed to stay undrugged and they even remembered to feed us once or twice a day. Then, whether day or night we couldn't tell, the ship suddenly shuddered as if applying brakes and thumped gently against something solid. We were there.

CHAPTER SEVEN

I t wasn't a major dock, just some jetty in a small bay and a peasant village behind it circled by steep jungled mountains. They let us up on deck, Jeff and me, and didn't seem to mind a bit that a couple of customs officials saw us. If you've been paid enough to ignore even smuggled guns, I suppose selective blindness sets in and no eye doctor can cure you.

Crate after crate moved out of the guts of the ship onto decrepit trucks that took the contraband away on a dirt road into the surrounding jungle. If there were weapons in those big boxes, Hector would soon be able to equip a couple of thousand men.

No one seemed to be paying much attention to us, and I entertained the thought of flipping a signal to Jeff and then trying to make a break for it. But common sense spoiled the fun. If a big ship could tie up at this jetty and off-load tons of suspicious crates, no doubt the rebels had the whole town in their pocket. Besides, we were probably now in Juanita. Not counting the rebels who had brought us there and the president who had tried to have me killed, who could we rely on to be friendly?

"Nice scene," Jeff said beside me, looking across at the village ringing the bay.

"In what way?"

"I don't know. It's kind of picturesque, like out of some pirate movie."

"It's a rebel stronghold and you're a doomed prisoner. How picturesque is that?"

"You think I don't know we're in trouble?" he said, turning to me.

"Just stop romanticizing this. We need wits, not mush."

"We need God, not wits," he said. Touché.

After they'd left us in the sun for an hour or two, the air full of smells of fuel, foliage and a hint of decay, they loaded the last truck and sent it on its way. The ship's crew then wandered off into the village. A couple of thugs stayed behind on deck, presumably to watch over us, though they kept their distance while they talked quietly to one another and smoked.

So what was the plan? Why us? Why here? The more I thought about it, the more I suspected that Simpson had cut his rate on the armaments to the rebels in return for their help in making me disappear. Jeff was along only because he'd been in the wrong place at the wrong time. But why go through such an elaborate plan and take us all the way to Juanita when I could be just as dead in Canada?

A car suddenly shot out of the jungle, coming from the direction the trucks had taken. It headed straight toward the ship at top speed and braked beside the jetty in a swirl of dust. The cavalry coming to save us? Not likely. Someone got out of the back of it, and I recognized Hector, commander of the rebels. He wasted no time in walking up the gangplank onto the deck of our ship.

"Mr. Sylvester," he said in Spanish, coming toward us. "It's good to see you again." Jeff looked puzzled at the warmth of the greeting.

"Why?" I asked.

"Excuse me?" Hector asked.

"Why is it good for you to see me?"

"I presume your question demands a deep answer. Let me just say for now that we see you as an ally. You've proven how much you despise the schemes of our president."

"Your people kidnapped us."

The "us" made him turn his head to Jeff. "Who is this?"

"They didn't tell you?"

"No."

"Jeff here is a friend of mine. He made the mistake of trying to protect me." I beckoned to Hector, and we moved out of earshot of the thugs. "Look," I said, "my friend Jeff doesn't understand any of this. Put him across the border like you did for me."

"It's too late for that," Hector said. "Unless your friend is very ignorant, he has a good understanding of what must have been in those crates we sent into the jungle."

I knew it was a lost cause. "Why are we here, then? If I'm such a great ally—"

"You are. We need your help."

"Ben?" Jeff said, coming toward us. "What's going on?"

"If you'll have a little patience, I'll find out for you, OK?" I said. Hector gave the hint of a smile. "What do you want from me?" I asked him.

"I suppose I owe you that much for all the inconvenience you have suffered." Inconvenience? "You were brought here to help us formulate a public face to the world."

"A what?"

"We are virtually an unknown movement, very young. Unknown movements need to create external sympathies. If you believe in our cause, then help us create an image that the world will appreciate."

Hector had an in-charge look to him in his army fatigues, dark hair and mustache, tough physique, that wide flat face. But I couldn't conceive how a rational man would have kidnapped someone then expected his victim to gladly help him advertise his cause to the world.

"I don't like your president, but I detest armed revolutionaries almost as much," I said. He only smiled.

"Where does that leave us, Mr. Sylvester?" he said quietly. "Would money be an encouragement?"

"No."

"Threats? Torture?"

"I'd rather you didn't."

"Let's leave it there for now," he said. Hector, Jeff, and I got into his car, a fully restored 1955 Ford that came with its own driver. As we headed into the jungle, Jeff gave me a look of exasperation. I let him stew while we bumped along deteriorating roads, moving rapidly away from the coast.

Hector sat in the back between Jeff and me, his eyes closed, his body oblivious to the jolting. From the other side of him, Jeff mouthed questions at me, but I've never been any good at lip-reading.

Rats in a trap. They say the best way to finish them off is to hold the whole trap under water for a few minutes. As we moved deeper into the jungle, I imagined I could hear water gurgling just under my chin.

After an hour of travel, we spotted an armed man standing at the side of the road. He pulled aside a clever foliage-covered barrier, and we drove into a cleared area under the jungle canopy, the whole base invisible from the road and from the air.

This was a more permanent camp than the one I'd hidden in the last time I fled Juanita. The place sported five or six bamboo buildings and a windowless shed of rough board siding. The trucks that had carried our ship's cargo were grouped at the edge of the clearing. About three dozen men were busy unloading with hand-operated hooks and pulleys, all the boxes going into one of the bamboo buildings. Everything was hedged by jungle on steep hillsides, the air humid and utterly still in the heat. For my part, I longed for just one easy-strike match and a few seconds of freedom.

Hector didn't waste much time bundling us into his office in another one of the buildings. There wasn't much there to indicate his status—a battered table, a lamp that ran off the generator, five or six wooden chairs. He sat us down and pulled his own chair close, sitting on it backwards, with his arms draped over the upright.

"We have much to organize here," he said in Spanish. "But first—" He paused, then quickly turned his head to stare at Jeff. "Who is this man?" He tone was soft, but the menace was hard to miss.

"He's an old friend of mine. Used to be a librarian," I said.

"What is he now?"

"A friend. He works in a factory."

"Mr. Sylvester." Hector turned his head back to me, his eyes cutting laser holes in my face. "Your answer might satisfy a fool, but I am not a fool. Who is he?"

"What's he saying, Ben?" Jeff asked.

"He wants to know who you are. I told him you're a friend."

"Tell him the truth."

"What?"

"Tell him."

Hector's eyes flickered.

"Jeff is an untrained informant for the Canadian Security

Intelligence Service," I said in Spanish.

"What does this agency have to do with me?" he asked.

"How should I know?"

"Ask him."

I did, but Jeff had decided to reveal no more. A few flies buzzed in the room, giving a feel of decadence to the already shabby office, and I wondered whether I'd just thrown my friend to the wolves.

Hector smiled at me. "We could beat this man or leave him tied near an ant colony," he said, "but he would probably lie to me, since I cannot verify his information. If I kill him, you will probably become even more difficult."

"I never agreed to help you," I said. "'Most any revolutionary I've ever met is a power-seeker."

"You have rather limited choices, Mr. Sylvester. Help me or suffer the consequences."

"Did you learn that line in rebel school? Look, a few months ago a certain African governor made much the same speech to me, except that he wanted me to work on a coup with him. He's dead now."

"Am I supposed to be frightened by that?"

"Just a friendly warning that people like you tend to self-destruct."

"I will have plans to unveil in the morning," he said, getting up abruptly. "Please be alert when I call for you, because I have little patience these days."

He put us into the shed with the thinly planked roof and walls, barred window, armed guard outside the door. The small metal camp beds that virtually filled the room looked like a poor prospect for restful sleep.

When the door slammed shut, Jeff sat down precariously on

the edge of one of them and said, "You've really put us in the soup this time, Ben."

"Me?" I said. "You're the one who's too clumsy to be sent off to stalk people in the woods. And why didn't you tell me how dangerous it was to meet that guy Pancho?"

"I didn't know until it was too late. Why do you keep harping on it?"

It was clear from his uneasiness that Jeff knew what I was going to ask him next: "This is the time when you tell me everything about everything," I said. "Things will get rough for you if you don't." My look, I hoped, was intimidating.

"I'm not supposed to know anything."

"But?"

"They accidentally left a document in the room with me when they were getting ready to sign me on with CSIS. I was alone for half an hour. Boy, were they mad when they saw me reading it."

"What did it say?"

"I can't tell you." He saw my face tightening. "I can't tell you, Ben. I made a promise."

"Forget promises. I intend to get out of this, and you have to tell me what you know."

"You need to pray, Ben. This isn't something we can fight our way out of."

"It's both-and, not either-or. God doesn't take well to bailing out fools."

"It won't help you to know my secrets."

"Let me be the judge."

"OK." He looked at the floor.

"First tell me what Harry Simpson's scheme is."

"He..." Jeff stopped, his eyes pleading for a reprieve.

"Tell me or—"

"Simpson realized a long time ago that there were opportunities with the kind of work he was doing. Shaky democratic movements, people wondering if violence wouldn't put them further ahead, other people looking to put down movements before their own dictatorships got blasted."

"So he offered extra services and he didn't much care who he worked for," I said. "What's he into exactly?"

"A few times early on he betrayed rebel movements to the people in power. Then he branched out, mainly into spy-for-hire and gunrunning."

"Things such as supplying guns to the rebels of Juanita or helping an African governor get expertise for a coup attempt?"

"Or hiring a South American to knife you and networking with Middle Eastern spies to infiltrate your father-in-law's electronics company."

"But he never tried to recruit me."

"He thinks you're stupid, easily used. He did try to have you killed on that South American job, but only because the plot he was working on needed you out of the way. When you escaped alive, he went back to using you."

"How did CSIS find out?" I asked him, feeling waves of anger, not knowing what to do with it.

"FBI. Simpson made some dumb moves in the past few years and they've been watching him, hoping to net a whole bunch of other people when they finally reel him in."

I was chilled by a sudden thought, and I hid it by walking over to the heavily barred window. It was starting to rain outside.

"What?" Jeff said.

"Nothing. I have to work it out."

"Tell me."

I mulled it over a few seconds, then explained. "Simpson has his hooks into the rebels here. He also has ties to the president of Juanita."

"So?"

"So where do we fit into this?"

"You're supposed to help Hector run an advertising campaign to win worldwide sympathy for his cause."

"Too simple. Anyone could do that for him. Why kidnap me out of Canada? And what's he going to do with us when I've taught him all I know?"

"Kill us," Jeff said. "Otherwise you'd repudiate everything you did for him as soon as you were free."

"So why didn't he find someone more sympathetic to his cause, someone he wouldn't have to eliminate?"

"Maybe Simpson wants to get rid of you because he suspects you're on to him."

"It would have been easier to leave us at the bottom of Harrison Lake. Hector doesn't need me. There are lots of people around who could help him advertise. I don't even like revolutionaries. Simpson knows that."

Later, someone brought some passable food for us and when darkness came we fell into an uneasy sleep. I dreamed that Karen was speaking to me, but the only word she said was trust. Over and over—"trust, trust, trust." She wasn't afraid.

CHAPTER EIGHT

I n my dream I ran silently in the darkness, feeling the sky very close above me, my feet finding the path so easily that I must have been guided by someone unseen. Then the clouds parted in a V, and moonlight pushed past them like a glistening sword, and I saw the one who had been leading me, and I was surprised that I knew him.

He turned to speak to me as we ran, his voice coming from him like a gentle roar, a subdued whirring. I couldn't discern any distinction of words. His sound grew louder until it filled my mind, and I found myself lying on a cot—not running—on a cot in a planked room. But the muffled whirring sound went on.

I saw nothing, the darkness virtually complete in our tiny building after we'd fastened the window shutter for the night against potential snakes. The sound I'd heard was jungle noise— frogs and insects signaling that a cloudburst was probably on the way. Fumbling, I found the catch for the shutter and opened it, aware of the strong bars that still blocked any possible escape.

Slightly cooler air, velvet with humidity, floated in. I could see a few stars, even a half-moon through the scattered clouds.

Around the clearing, the trees were black. Behind them the mountains formed an immense amphitheater.

"Ben?" Jeff said, his voice muzzy.

"Sorry. Needed some air. Go back to sleep."

"On this cot? Not likely."

"Want to tell me more about CSIS secrets?"

"Not really."

I turned and looked at his form, now dimly visible with my growing night vision. "Why do I have the impression that you know more than you told me?"

"There's..." His voice trailed off.

"No," I said. "No, not again." I grabbed a handful of his shirt.

"I hardly know a thing."

"Why do you always do this to me?"

"Do what?"

I let go of the shirt. "Don't hide things from me. Whatever misbegotten loyalty you have for the people you work for doesn't cut it here."

"OK."

"OK, so?"

"The secret. We...uh..." He swallowed. "We learned that the leader of the coca growers of Colombia was actually one of Hector's rebels."

"I gathered that. But you guys knew about it before you let me walk into the trap?" His look confirmed it. "What else?"

"The president of Juanita has a spy among the rebels, someone close to Hector."

"You're kidding. How do you know?" He looked at the ceiling. "Jeff?"

"They...they said that if you should happen to be captured by the rebels, and I should happen to be with you, one of us should know about the spy."

"Why would they think I was going to be captured?"

"Because they've bugged Harry Simpson's office, and his car and who knows what else. That's how they found out your coca grower was actually a rebel. Simpson wanted you captured. The only mistake my people made was assuming you wouldn't be snatched the first time you met the guy."

"It wasn't a mistake," I said. "Your people set us up."

"Why would they do that?"

"They're not really interested in some rebel from Juanita. They want to throw the book at Simpson."

"Are you trying..." He paused, confusion on his face. "They deliberately let us be captured because they wanted to follow us here?"

"Didn't need to follow us. The Juanitan president has a pipeline from this base."

"So CSIS and the FBI are working with the ruler of Juanita?" The outrage in his voice was laughable.

"Join the real world, OK?" I said. "They're trying to land an illegal arms dealer and all-round dirty trickster. Getting chummy with the president of Juanita is part of the dues you pay." It's easy to spin out an explanation if you don't have all the facts. I only wish I'd been more accurate in my guesses.

We fell back into jumbled sleep, neither of us going deep enough to be rested. About seven, one of the rebels came in and nudged us roughly awake. We filed out, still in the same dirty clothes, and were led to an outdoor table with some bread and fruit on it.

From where I sat munching on a juicy thing I never learned the name of, I could see men occupied in various tasks, carrying sacks and water jugs, bedrolls and a few old rifles, everything looking like anarchy. All of Hector's men had a certain rough practical look to them.

As we finished our breakfast, Hector came up, smiling. "I hope you are rested," he said to me. "You will need to use that keen mind of yours a great deal today."

"What did he say?" Jeff asked.

"He said he needs me but he doesn't need you. So I guess you have to occupy yourself. Sorry."

Hector led me into another building where a big table was set up. On the table were a number of rough pamphlets and brochures, pen-and-ink things in layout form. All of them detailed atrocities in Juanita and called for reforms. All of them were stamped, "Citizen's Freedom Party."

"Who put these together?" I asked.

"Me," Hector said, his voice showing some pride. "I was a commercial artist and writer before the oppression of my people became too much for me to bear."

"What do you want from me?"

"To go through this work from the viewpoint of a political advisor. Some of my men tell me I'm too much of a romantic to appeal to the hard hearts of westerners. Our goal is to bring economic sanctions against Juanita."

"Your goal," I said, "is to overthrow the president by force. The advertising is only intended to win western sympathy for the bloodbath."

"Violence is a last resort only," he said. "We are well aware, Mr. Sylvester, of the history of revolution in this part of the world, pain brought by movements such as the Sandinistas and Shining Path: all those foolish Marxists with stars in their eyes. I have no burning desire to bring that pain back to Juanita."

I stared at him, trying to picture him as the head of a violent revolt. Hector on the surface seemed too civilized for the role.

"Do I have your assurance that you only want me to help you get the record of abuses out to the West? I won't be part of any revolution."

He smiled and gave me his assurances.

I learned that the country known as Juanita had its start with the arrival of the Conquistadors looking for gold and not concerned about who they took it from. Their successors saw opportunities in sugar and cattle. To further their aims, the king of Spain gave them huge land grants and permission to use the native population as feudal serfs.

The Catholic Church, also a major landholder, showed some concern for the plight of the Indian farmers who were generally poor and servile. To encourage them and ease the sting of their situation, the priests taught the natives that it was God who had given them their lowly station in life, and they should rejoice in this gift they had received at his hand.

Certainly, there were minor rebellions over the years, but each was crushed by the ever-vigilant military. Only with the 1970s did the powers in the land begin to fear. Miguel Santos, a village priest, began preaching about the abuses he had observed. He stressed God's love for the poor and hatred of the oppressor, and his congregation, energized by hope, spread his message to the rest of the country. Miguel was eventually drawn into a Marxist movement, there was a brief flurry of terrorism, then the army destroyed the whole thing, killing Miguel in the process.

Hector, in one of his brochures, took up his own story:

We of the universities were lost and uncomprehending, more concerned about dancing and drunken parties than about the cruelty of the reprisals that followed the martyrdom of Miguel. For myself, I thought of nothing but pleasure and my own career as a great artist or perhaps a poet. Then one day my best friend Carlos disappeared. He had said the wrong thing in the hearing of the wrong person. I never saw him again.

You who read this account must understand that we who fight are not legendary heroes riding on the clouds for a noble cause. We are simply men who have been sleeping and have been shocked into wakefulness by personal pain.

That is why you must believe our stories and join us in the battle to bring freedom to our land. We have been sleeping, but no one can rest any longer when his friend has been taken. No one can sleep again as long as tyrants gloat and the poor die.

I had to give him credit. Hector could certainly turn a phrase or two.

CHAPTER NINE

I watched her eyes mostly because there was nothing in them, as if somebody had vacuumed away her life and left her only breathing, moving, talking. She was about thirty-five, attractive if you didn't look into her eyes. I'd heard her story many times in many places.

"And they came as they had promised," she was saying. "Five of them—big men—they came for my husband who would not have lifted a stick to strike a mouse. They took him, he vanished, but through the night in my mind I could hear his screams until my thoughts told me that he could no longer be living."

"What had he done?" I asked.

"He spoke out against the young man who struck our child. The young man has a father in the army."

"What had your child done to anger the man?"

"Nothing. The young man struck him because his father was in the army, and he knew he could."

Hector had brought her. When she got up from her chair in the clearing, the next one in line took her place and told me his story, then the next. Every account was virtually a duplicate of the one before.

I found myself absorbing their pain, not surprised by it but wondering that it clung to me so fiercely. The president, to put it gently, led a pack of monsters motivated only by greed and power. By the end of the day, I was wishing I had a remote control for the thunderbolts of heaven.

Which was exactly what Hector wanted. So I asked him, after everyone had gone, "Why were Jeff and I kidnapped?" I had to get to the depths of the man and find out what he was capable of doing about the horrors of his land.

"It was a condition of our arms purchase," he said. "We were told—"

"By Harry Simpson."

"By the man who sold us the arms that you were to be removed from North America. He said it would be easy to persuade you to help us."

"Why was I to be removed from North America?"

Hector shrugged. "There was never an explanation. He simply said that if we wanted the arms we had to bring you here. I objected, of course, but there was no choice. He said we were to keep you two months, then release you over the border as we did the last time you were here."

"And Jeff?"

"A surprise to us. My men felt compelled to bring him too or everyone would have known how you disappeared."

"Now my family thinks I drowned on Harrison Lake," I said. "Thank you very much."

"It was out of my hands."

"Why would Harry Simpson want you to release me in two months? He knows I'll go back to the States and expose him."

"Perhaps he intends to flee the country."

"If I was dead, he might not have a reason to flee."

Hector stared at me for a few seconds. "It seems to me that you have better answers to your questions than I do," he said.

"How do you figure that?"

"Because you know much more about this than you've told me." I could have denied it, but he was too smart for that.

"Honestly, Hector, I don't know how much to tell you," I said. "Give me some time to think."

He let me wander around for a while. In my travels through the compound, I found Jeff looking bored, whittling with a dull pocketknife someone had foolishly left lying around. As near as I could see, Jeff was about to bless the camp with a year's supply of toothpicks.

The big hole in my understanding was growing by the minute. It came down to this—if the president of Juanita had a mole right next to Hector, then the Juanitan government knew everything about Hector's organization. Why then had the brave army of Juanita not mopped up the rebels long since? What were they waiting for?

This was more than I could even begin to unravel. I went around the corner of a building, out of sight, and spent some time communing with the only One who could possibly know everything that was going on. Gradually calming myself as I went over it with him, I started to listen—not to words (I'm not into divine revelation at the drop of a hat), just a sense of direction through the fog.

After about twenty minutes I went looking for Hector and found him snoozing under a tree. To test his reflexes, I kicked him lightly in the leg. No sudden movement. He just slowly opened his eyes and gave me a look of mild annoyance.

"OK, I'll tell you the rest," I said, sitting down at an angle to him, leaning against the same tree. He shut his eyes again. "Your band of merry men includes at least one government informant," I said.

"Nonsense."

"True."

"I've known every person in this camp for many years."

"Then one of them has sold you out. Someone close to you." I looked out across the compound where dozens of men were exercising, resting, loading backpacks.

"Why hasn't the army already attacked us if they know everything?" he said.

"I don't know."

"Could you tell me how you obtained this information?"

"No."

"If such a traitor exists, what's he waiting for?"

"I have no idea."

"You'll need sleep," he said, getting up abruptly. "Tomorrow I want you to start working on revisions for my pamphlets. They have to be published within three weeks."

"And the informant?"

"Is not your concern." He walked away, leaving me still leaning against the palm tree. I went looking for Jeff again. He wasn't happy that I'd given so much away to Hector, which was why I hadn't consulted with him before I did it.

I spent the next day going over Hector's advertising. The main thrust of it was the abuses of the Juanitan army, but it also revealed enough about Juanita's stifled democratic yearnings to bring out the righteous indignation of virtually anyone. It was rough hewn stuff, poetic, flowery, emotional, but not focused enough to move the hearts and minds of the cynical West. I tweaked his material for him making it more of a lunge for the jugular. From what I'd heard the day before, his allegations of human rights abuses deserved every chance to be heard.

But I'd always opposed violent politics of every stripe. When you raise a gun, you sacrifice, measure by measure, your ability to champion the rational motives behind your cause. All the grays either wash out into white or dirty themselves into black. Eventually you're reduced to the options of angry schoolboys in an alley in the late afternoon.

That was why, at the end of the day, watching Jeff in the distance busy at whittling again, I called Hector over, showed him what editing I'd done, and went on strike.

"You can't," he said, his face showing anger. "That is simply not possible."

"I did what you asked me to do," I said.

"A larger task is ahead. I've written a book."

"You want me to read it, do some editing?"

"It's only about 150 pages of manuscript."

"And how do you intend to get it published?"

"Publishers will fight with one another for the opportunity to produce my work." His look warned me not to challenge him.

"How far along are you?"

"One complete draft. It needs revision."

"I'm honored, Hector, really, but this is starting to look like a long-term relationship. I've done enough."

"Did you leave your mind floating in the clouds when those victims of our president came here yesterday and told you what happened to them?"

"I sympathize. But the path you've chosen will only demean you."

"You are speaking of the guns?"

"I won't help you anymore, Hector."

"Can't you accept my explanation that the guns are only to

give us courage and defend us from the army?"

"No."

"Perhaps when the whole world reads my book, the one you will edit for me, we will get the economic sanctions we need without having to resort to guns."

"Look, Hector," I said. "Pay attention. The Juanitan army knows where you are. It knows you have armaments. I have no idea what your beloved president is waiting for, but the sky is going to fall on you very soon."

There was no arguing with him. He sent me off to bed, and the next morning, sensitive to the glares of Jeff who was going quietly insane from boredom, I found Hector and asked him to give me his manuscript.

The book wasn't too bad, really. He had a gift for expressing himself, for painting a scene. It was a history of the poor and oppressed of Juanita, a bit rambling, too emotional in places, but definitely worth something to a publisher.

I didn't want to help him anymore. I couldn't get past the fact that his last resort was revolution. But I found myself reading the manuscript with interest, writing a few notes in the margins, then more notes. Lunch came and I scarcely noticed what I was eating until the peppers started burning in my throat.

CHAPTER TEN

Coming out of exhausted sleep that night, I heard some-one fumbling at the door, then it opened and a dim fig-ure came in and whispered, "Hsst!"

"What?" Jeff said.

The intruder moved quickly to Jeff's bunk, presumably to silence him, then I was conscious enough to bolt up and grab the man from behind, circling his elbows with a bear hug.

"Let go," he whispered. "It's Hector."

I hesitated a few seconds, then let him go. "What's the idea?"

"Get dressed, both of you."

"What time is it?"

"Just before dawn. I need the two of you now."

"What for?" Jeff whispered.

"I'll tell you on the way. Hurry and dress."

When we went out, the camp was still in silence except for a few shadowy sentries. Hector guided us to one of the big trucks that had loaded the armaments off our ship, then he climbed into the driver's seat and motioned for us to join him in the cab.

The noise of the truck starting was enough to wake the deep-est sleeper. Ramming the truck into gear, Hector barreled us out of camp, turning on the headlights when we reached the road.

"Where are we going?" Jeff asked as we bumped along a dirt track that was starting to ascend. I noticed a few raindrops hitting the windshield.

"We're going to trap a spy," Hector said.

"You told me you didn't believe in spies," I said.

He laughed. "Often the best way to get information out of a man is to claim you don't believe him."

"The spy's not out here," Jeff said. "He's still back in your camp."

"But our guns are out here. Ben, you asked me why the president's forces have not yet attacked us. It's because we haven't yet brought our guns into the camp. The army knows it would be a public relations disaster to massacre poorly armed men."

"But we saw you unloading crates in the camp," I said.

"Only food and other supplies. We hid the guns in the forest."

"Why?" The truck began to bounce through a series of potholes just as a downpour hit us.

"Let me concentrate," he said. "This road is very bad."

"You knew about the spy before I told you."

"Suspected." He swung the truck hard to the right to avoid a deep pool, then corrected. "That's why we hid the guns. Emilio, my second in command, will go to a town this afternoon. He is supposed to be buying me a typewriter, but I believe he will also meet a government representative and tell him where the guns are hidden."

"Then the army will seize your weapons."

"Not at first. They'll send a few men to determine that the location is accurate. I've told Emilio that we'll move the guns to the camp next week. That's when the army will attack us, probably just as we're unpacking."

It was getting lighter as we drove along the steep mountain slope, palm trees above and below us. The truck was underpowered and labored heavily, nearly stalling several times. If anything, the road was getting bumpier, its edges crumbling in some places.

"What made you suspect Emilio?" Jeff asked.

"He used to talk constantly about his wife and three small children. Suddenly one day about two months ago he stopped. His whole manner became peculiar after he visited a village to get supplies. When I asked him why he was no longer boring us with endless family memories, he said he'd finally learned that some things were too precious to talk about."

"What does that mean?" Jeff said.

"It means," I said, "that the army got to Emilio's family."

The rain stopped about the time I decided we must have bypassed the beanstalk and found the land of the giants another way. As the mists cleared, I saw that we had nearly reached the top of the world. Below us I could see forty or fifty miles of jungle, with the seacoast beyond.

Then Hector swung the truck to the right, as if he wanted to fly us off the edge of the embankment. Instead, there was a rough narrow path, partially overgrown.

A quarter of a mile along, we stopped. Through the bush, I could see a trail to rock outcropping. The path was wide enough for a small car but too narrow for the truck.

"There are handcarts in the back," Hector said. "We must hurry. The rain has delayed us."

We each took a cart, and Jeff and I followed Hector up the path. There was a cave in the rock about ten feet high, maybe six feet wide, twenty deep. In the back of it, lit by Hector's flashlight, were about forty crates ranging in size from a big suitcase to a small fridge. It might have been cool in the cave, but I knew the heat and humidity outside were already moving beyond the comfort zone for heavy labor.

Jeff and I didn't really need to discuss the options. Whatever Hector was planning, he was hoping to foil the spy and avert an attack on our camp. Simple self-preservation made helping him the only choice.

It took us two or three hours to load the guns into the truck. The smaller boxes were all right, a couple of hundred pounds at the most. But the bigger ones were real killers. We almost gave up on one of them right at the truck because the three of us couldn't lift it the required four feet. Finally Hector rigged a rope to the winch on the front of the truck, tossed the rope over the length of the truck and hoisted the crane mechanically.

Hector hadn't spoken much during our labors but as we got into the truck he smiled at me and said, "Very good work. Half done." Jeff's face told me he appreciated Hector's humor even less than I did.

We rejoined the dirt road, then climbed over the mountain into a valley and up another slope that was steeper than any we'd encountered. Hector parked at the side of the road right at the top.

"You planning to dump the stuff over the side?" I asked.

"No, there's a secret trail over there." He pointed. I couldn't see anything but bush, but when we got out the handcarts there was a path that ran at an angle to the road. This time our destination at the end of the trail was a bamboo shed with a thatched roof, one door, no windows.

The smaller crates went into the shed, but the two biggest ones had to be left behind it under plastic tarps. By the end the three of us were utterly thrashed, and my leg was throbbing.

Hector had brought food, but he didn't share it with us until the last crate was loaded. Then we ate greedily. I hoped the day's efforts had been worth the wages of pain and sweat.

"Can we go home now?" I asked Hector.

"To America or to my encampment?" he asked.

"We'll take your place for now," Jeff said.

"I'm sorry. You'll have to sleep in the forest tonight. We set up camp near the place where I first stored the guns." He didn't like the glares we gave him. "It's important. If Emilio has told them where the guns were, they will send a small contingent tomorrow to verify the hiding place. We have to act as observers."

I should have been thinking of escape. Knock Hector on the head, steal his truck and head for the border, wherever that was. But I couldn't see myself just dumping Hector in the jungle, not when his men back in the camp had no idea how compromised they were because of the spy.

We followed the narrow track back to the rock outcropping and the cave where we'd picked up the guns. Hector drove another half mile beyond until the track ended. Then we used machetes to cut down undergrowth and cover the truck before we walked back to the cave with some camping gear Hector had brought along. Hector also carried a rifle with a scope that he'd pulled from under the truck seat.

"For safety," he explained.

While we set ourselves up in a craggy area above the cave, Hector went back over the road down to the truck, sweeping the mud with a palm branch. It was nearly dark when he joined us.

"I hope you'll be comfortable," he said. "You North Americano's love your camping."

I was hurting too much to enjoy the joke with him. "So you say the army will send some people tomorrow. What if they spot us?"

"And what if I condemn the wrong man?" Hector said. "Today is the first time since the guns arrived that I have given Emilio freedom. If no soldiers appear, then my suspicions are for nothing. Do you think I want to believe that my good friend has betrayed me?"

"The question I asked didn't call for a speech," I said.

"Save the grumpy mood, Ben," Jeff said. "When I was a kid I used to dream of camping out in the jungle."

"You're still a kid." I regretted it as soon as I said it, but Jeff didn't seem to notice. He and Hector got into a discussion about the ins and outs of night creatures. I nursed my mood.

Maybe it was simply the tiredness. Maybe it was because my leg was aching and I knew we hadn't brought painkillers. Or maybe I just needed to grow up myself.

It was hard to think that by now Karen would be convinced I was dead, drowned while fishing on Harrison Lake. Or it might have been that someone spotted us being transported to the plane. Whatever she'd been told, it wasn't fair after all the things she'd suffered because of me.

We finally got ourselves bedded down and we slept to the music of the night creatures.

Morning. I was well used to the amazing tropical transformation that turns day to night or night to day in less than half an hour. What I wasn't prepared for was the blazing sunrise that reflected off the clouds in oranges and purples. It had rained hard for a while during the night, but the day promised better things. The jungle smells—living vegetation mixed with decay—were strong in our nostrils.

The crag we'd camped on was about fifty feet above the mouth of the cave. Bushes growing out of the shallow soil gave us ample cover. We ate a cold breakfast and then waited.

By nine o'clock the humidity had risen to near saturation point, and we could see a big storm coming in. Hector kept looking at his watch and then at the clouds.

The soldiers came at nine-thirty. One jeep navigated the path to the cave, undergrowth slapping at its sides. Four men. One of them shouted an order and the other three went into the cave, stayed for a few minutes, then came out and reported.

Their commander must have been a hard man to work under. In the course of his harangue over the missing guns, he also explained in clinical detail what he planned to do to Emilio. I looked at Hector, expecting to see triumph on his face. Instead, there were tears.

"What now?" I whispered.

"Wait," he said. "We'll let them go."

The soldiers climbed into their jeep and backed out to the main track. Then one of them spotted something, and they all got out again.

"They're heading down toward our truck," Jeff whispered. "You didn't hide it well en—"

Just before the soldiers passed out of our vision behind the trees, the rest of Jeff's sentence was cut off by four rifle blasts. Amazed, I watched each soldier drop in sequence as if performing some avant-garde ballet. But the blood that flew everywhere put a lid on any notion that this was make believe. One of the soldiers twitched a few seconds, then was still. The others didn't move again at all.

Hector put down his rifle and wiped his hand over his face. He'd been kneeling, but now he sat and clasped his knees with his arms.

"Did you have to do that?"

"They would have found the truck, then us, then the guns.

After that, my men would be massacred. It used to be, Ben, that shooting was a diversion only. In university I became shooting champion for pleasure." He got up suddenly, then was violently sick over the embankment.

Eventually we climbed down, rain starting to fall. Before we could get the truck out, we had to move two of the bodies. Jeff thought of hiding all the evidence in the jungle, but it was clear that investigators would easily have found traces of what had happened there.

In the end, we left them on the ground. Even now I dream about it, the bodies lying in the rain while the thunder announces some kind of verdict.

e traveled in silence except for the rattling of the old truck now that it was virtually empty, now that we were going three times as fast as we'd climbed the road up the mountain the day before. Our main worry was that we had no idea when the now-dead soldiers had been expected to check in with their headquarters. There was only one road over the next thirty miles. A roadblock would be easy if the army suspected that its patrol had run into trouble.

I tried to concentrate on praying, but nasty images kept flashing into my mind. My stomach felt like someone had tied a clove hitch into it, and I was strangely cold. About twenty minutes into our descent of the mountain, I started to shiver.

"What's wrong?" Jeff asked.

"Cold. Close the windows." The windows went up, blocking the spray from the rain that was still falling. Then we started to fog and they had to roll the windows back down.

"You're not looking good," Jeff said.

"Not feeling good." It was as if some monster had invaded my body and was shoving it around. So cold. "Give me a blanket," I said.

"There's one behind the seat," Hector said. Jeff got it out and I wrapped myself in it.

It did no good. I'd never been so cold. My thoughts, I knew, were becoming disjointed, like the moments before sleep, and I fought to focus them.

"He has fever," Hector said, not taking his eyes off the road.

"It comes on that fast?" Jeff asked.

"Certainly. There is some Chloroquine in the box by your feet. It's old but it should work. Give him four tablets."

I dropped the first one as soon as Jeff handed it to me, so he ended up having to pop them in my mouth. The taste was so bad I nearly brought them up again. All I wanted was to still the shaking and melt the ice forming inside me.

We passed a village but saw no police, no soldiers. Maybe the detail Hector had killed hadn't been set up to communicate anything until they got back to headquarters. We could only hope.

After an hour of driving, the road branched and we were able to take another route than the one we'd come up on—more convoluted but less likely to bring us into contact with the wrong people. Hector seemed to know the area blindfolded.

For a while my shivering quieted and the edge came off the painful cold. Then everything got very warm very fast.

I pushed the blanket away. Now the ice monster turned into a beast of molten heat, grabbing me by the back of the neck and throwing me into a cauldron. I'd seen other people with tropical fevers, but I'd never believed it could become this much of a personal battle.

As we drove, I started losing touch in earnest, my mind drifting often, coming back and seeing only more jungle whizzing past. At one point I heard Jeff say, "He's really sick," and something about "any hospitals?" Hector gave an angry reply and we kept on driving.

The rest of the day is pretty much a jumble in my memory. Jeff told me later that I fell asleep and I only half woke up when we reached the camp. I remember only that we stopped for a while then started driving again on a very rough road.

Later that night, after we'd stopped again—at least I think it was that night—I remember hearing screams, like a man or a large animal in extreme pain. After a while it was quiet again.

Daylight, and a sunbeam woke me as it shone through the tent-flap. I didn't remember getting into a tent. When I climbed out of the bedroll and crawled to the entrance, I saw that I wasn't in Hector's camp.

"This isn't Kansas anymore, Toto," I mumbled to myself, feeling like porridge in a bowl. There seemed to be no fever, but I was unbelievably weak and I could feel the monster lurking.

Outside were three jeeps and four tents plus mine in a small clearing in the bush. Palm trees all around blocked everything but the sky and the sun. I could hear men's voices behind my tent.

Then Jeff showed up. "You're awake."

"In a manner of speaking," I said.

"How are you feeling?"

"Terrible. A baby could push me over."

"Hector told me it will be a week before you get your strength back."

"What's happening?"

"Most of the men have left for their homes. The rest packed up and now we're here."

"Where?"

"How should I know? Somewhere along the coast."

"Those screams I heard last night."

Jeff looked at the ground. "They needed information from Emilio."

"Torture? Where is he now?"

"Search me."

"I thought Hector had all those high ideals."

"He does. I heard him throwing up after. Actually it was his men that did the work on Emilio. I could hear Hector telling them they were going too far."

"I need to talk to him," I said, crawling out of the tent, then trying to stand. Jeff had to help me get upright. I noticed that my bad leg felt strange, maybe inflamed.

"Can you walk?"

"Not well."

He found a stick and I used it to get across the clearing to where Hector and his men were discussing the meaning of their lives.

Hector looked up at me. "You survived the night. That's very good."

"What are you planning?" I asked, sitting down on a log.

"Emilio has exposed most of our hiding places. I sent many of my men home. The rest of us are too well known to ever go home."

"And Emilio—where is he?"

"That is none of your concern."

"So are we just going to hide here until the army stops looking for you?"

"Go and rest, Ben," he said. "We'll speak later."

For two days I spent most of my time in the tent, generally sleeping, fighting the return of fever. They doctored me with Chloroquine but very little of my strength came back. My leg was swollen and sore. Hector ignored me, probably because he'd seen my look when I asked him about Emilio.

On the third day, Hector came into my tent and sat on the floor. "It is time to travel, Ben. The jeeps will take us most of the way. Are you strong enough?"

"Where to?"

"Across the border near the place you were put over the first time we met."

"When do we leave?"

"When I tell you. We are hoping the patrols will be smaller now that we have hidden for a while." He paused. "Emilio…"

"Yes?"

"Ben, this is not what I aspired to. I never wanted to be a guerrilla or to hurt anyone. They drove me to it."

"Is that how you comfort yourself?"

"Emilio must have had a weak heart. We questioned him—"

"Tortured him."

"I didn't want any of this."

"You made your choice," I said, "when you decided to fight your battle with guns." He got up and left.

The day passed as quietly as the previous two, but I felt little fever until evening. Then the monster returned just as Jeff came in to tell me to get out of the tent so he could pack it up.

When everything was loaded, Hector motioned for us to get into one of the jeeps. He drove it out onto a dirt road, and the convoy, with only the light of dimmed flashlights, followed him.

I'd been trying to hold it together, but now I found myself shivering, the last vestiges of whatever courage I had shaking out of me, my leg swollen and painful. I realized I'd been lying to myself ever since Africa, assuming that life goes on when you've been terrorized and shot and kidnapped and given a fever, assuming that you brush it off like crumbs on your lapel.

But you don't.

"Ben?"

"I'm all right."

"Take my sweater." Jeff draped it around my shoulders.

"We have two hours of travel left," Hector said.

"I'm all right."

"You're sick again," Jeff said.

"No."

Outside there was a glow in the air, more than just moon-light, a glow in the sky, and I could swear I saw angels flying past us, guiding our way, and I knew I was healthier than Hector or Jeff because I could see angels.

I woke hours later, a campfire burning near me, maybe too near. I was covered with blankets and sweating like a pig. Another clearing, jungle all around. Dawn coming fast, the vehicles in a half circle at the edge of the clearing. Vague shapes of men.

"Jeff?"

"Here." He leaned down over me. "I didn't think you'd be awake yet."

"Thirsty."

He brought me a bottle of warm Coke, and I choked on it, then sipped slowly until it was gone. I couldn't get up, though I did manage to prop myself on an elbow. Jeff put his fingers on my forehead.

"Fever's down," he said.

"Why…"

"Why what, Ben?"

"Why's this happening?" I felt anger that I wasn't home in bed, that I was sick and had to lie in a stinking jungle.

"Harry Simpson, that's why."

"Call him."

"Who, Simpson?"

"Hector."

Jeff went to get him while I shook my head and blinked hard, trying to focus, forcing my mind to ignore the images flitting at the edges of my brain. Hector came over after a while, his face showing concern.

"You must tell me what's happening," I said, panic growing because I couldn't understand much.

"You're still very sick," Hector said.

"Where are we going?"

"We're resting for the day. Tonight we cross the border. We'll find sanctuary until we can rebuild our movement."

I drifted off after that and they shoved me into a bedroll for the day. When I woke, it was dark again. The men were packing up, ready to move on. I was surprised at how strong I felt. When Jeff checked on me, he couldn't feel any sign of fever.

"Can you travel?" Hector asked me.

"I have to." Before they could help me, I climbed awkwardly out of the bedroll, wrapped it together, pushed it up onto one of the vehicles and got up into the jeep, breathing hard.

"Take it easy, Ben," Jeff said as he got in beside me.

"I'm fine."

"Your eyes are still too glazed."

"I'll be OK." I was jumpy, as if I'd spent the day drinking coffee.

"Only twenty minutes more of travel," Hector said. "They will give us no trouble at the border."

"Are you sure you have to leave the country?" I asked.

"If I don't they will hunt us down," he said. "We'll have freedom over there to promote my cause until it is safer here."

"What about the rest of your men?"

"Scattered. We have several means of leaving the country. Some have chosen to stay."

We were driving with lights now, clouds blocking the moon, jungle and darkness forming an eerie tunnel ahead of us.

"How much did the spy tell you?" I asked, not enjoying entering Hector's dusky world where treachery was met with detached torture and death.

"He revealed that the federals have known the locations of all of our encampments for weeks."

"Why in the world didn't they wipe you out before you got the guns?"

"That," he said, steering us carefully around a sharp bend, "is the secret the spy died for. The federals wanted us to have the guns because they are of American manufacture. When the soldiers would finally come to destroy us, they could claim that we had been armed by the CIA. Our president would tell the world that he was under attack from American imperialism, and this news would help him hold onto power."

"That doesn't explain why I was brought here," I said, my mind clear now, ready to deal with whatever he told me.

"Your Mr. Simpson is worried that the American authorities suspect him of running guns. He arranged for you to be in our camp when the president's soldiers attacked us. You would be blamed for selling us the guns and the president could claim that the Americans were supporting my plans for a coup."

"He doesn't know," Jeff said.

"Who?" I said.

"Harry Simpson doesn't know that I photographed him talking to that foreign agent in your mother-in-law's electronics company. He's got no idea that we've been on to him for months and for a lot more than gunrunning. The man thinks he's pinned everything on you and now he can go on as if nothing happened."

"Your people have to stop him then," I said.

"His people," Hector said, his voice icy. I didn't answer him. "Canadian intelligence."

We were silent for a minute or two while Hector drove hard, the others in the convoy dropping back.

"Jeff, you would have been even more of a coup for our beloved president than Ben was," Hector said finally. "Imagine, a Canadian intelligence officer found dead among the rebels of Juanita."

"He's not really an agent," I said, "and we're not dead."

"Which will make the president extremely angry, I'm sure."

"But we won't have any trouble at the border?"

"Not here. The officials on our side of it support our movement, and the country we are going to would love to have our president deposed."

Two more miles or so, and Hector slowed, his eyes searching the darkness for something, not seeing it. He frowned but said nothing, moving at a crawl now, turning off the flashlight he was using to guide us. Behind us, our convoy caught up and doused their lights too.

"What is it?" Jeff asked.

"They were to leave a lantern lit along the road so that we would know it is safe. Perhaps it has just gone out."

"Are you going to risk crossing anyway?"

"No." He shut off the motor and jumped down. "There is a trail to our right. It leads to the river. Wait for us there."

"Where are you going?" I asked.

"Ahead on foot. We must know if the crossing has been compromised."

"Hector," I said.

"What?"

"We'll pray for you."

"Please do," he said as he led his men in a scatter pattern up the road.

Jeff and I prayed for their safety as we stumbled down the trail, tripping on vines, hoping like crazy that our clumsiness would scare off the snakes. Within minutes we were both sweating, the humid air clinging to us. Once I caught my foot and fell hard, feeling the pain in my bad leg, pushing on anyway because we needed to get to the river.

Then the night erupted with gunfire, a full-scale battle to the left of us, fire and returning fire. It lasted about five minutes while we crouched in the bushes near the water. Finally there was only the sound of cries and groans. A single shot. Another. Yet another. Then someone screaming, then another shot. Silence.

CHAPTER TWELVE

H e was out of his league," I said. "Why do they always think that the stars in their eyes qualify—" I broke off, coughing.

"Rest, Ben," Jeff said. "We couldn't have saved him."

I stopped pacing in the narrow clearing next to the river and sat down, my back against a tree, not even bothering to check for snakes. Let them watch out for themselves.

Earlier, Jeff and I swam across the river without encountering either crocodiles or piranhas. We'd expected troops to be waiting on the other side, but we found no one in the clearing which had been cut out of the jungle and was sheltered from the slope above by the surrounding foliage. We decided to stay put until daylight.

I tried to sleep, but my thoughts intruded. Hector had seen warning signs that something nasty was waiting for him up ahead. That was why he'd sent us by the side trail. He had been basically a good man too much influenced by a desire to get the job done fast, and in the end he'd done things that sickened him. Why do the monsters always conclude that the best way to interact with good men is to devour them?

The biggest monster of them all, as far as I was concerned,

was back in Seattle. By now he would have heard that Jeff and I had escaped.

"Jeff," I said.

"What?" Sleepy voice.

"Simpson will know that we got free. He'll go after my family. I know him."

"They're not home." His words were slurred.

"Where—" Another coughing fit. My lungs felt like the inside of a blast furnace.

"They've been at Dave's house since we disappeared." Dave Mancuso, Jeff's pastor brother. I remembered their little house in Canada.

"How do you know that?" I said.

"I arranged it with Dave. If anything happened to you. Let me sleep."

You arranged it, did you, Jeff? Everyone arranges everything and all I have to do is roll with the punches. So much for the last vestiges of Ben Sylvester, control freak. But I was grateful.

I looked up into the sky, now cloud-free, the moon and stars so brilliant they dazzled the eye. "Is there really a plan to all this?" I said softly. "Is any of this going to bring some good to the world?"

"What?"

"Nothing, Jeff. Not talking to you."

"Go to sleep," he said.

I wonder what you'll let me do with Simpson. How would you like me to go about destroying this evil?

Why do you want to destroy him? What's your motive?

He put me through hell. He all but destroyed my family. He killed Hector.

The army killed Hector, who never should have taken to violence. He who lives by the sword—

What do you want me to do?

He didn't answer.

I slept for a while, horrors creeping at the edge of my thoughts, my body tortured by coughing and fever, dread growing because I was losing it and had just enough presence of mind left to know that I was losing it.

Morning. We were in a clearing ten feet across. Jeff was lying in a heap in the middle of it, and I was half sitting up, my back hard against a tree. I stared mindlessly for a while then slowly got up, my bad leg screaming at me. Looking around, I saw an opening in the jungle, a trail leading upward.

I kicked Jeff's foot. "Let's get going." He stirred and shook himself awake. "Trail over here."

"To where?"

"You want to stay down here until the snakes find us or the crocs smell an easy meal?"

Uneasily, we climbed the narrow trail, pushing aside heavy vines. A python slithered away. That didn't scare me nearly as much as the realization that the first soldier or cop who saw us coming up from the border might be tempted to shoot to wound first and torture later. I voiced my fears to Jeff.

"No, they won't," Jeff said, panting. "You're paranoid. We'll explain what happened and they'll take us to the U.S. embassy."

I was having a hard time of it, the fever and growing congestion in my chest making my heart work far too hard. Two hundred, three hundred feet of climb through encroaching undergrowth, and still we weren't at the end of it. They met us—eight or ten soldiers coming down out of nowhere. We hadn't heard them approaching. Jeff turned when he saw them, as if he doubted his own assurances to me, as if he wanted to bolt back to the river. I stood where I was.

"To your knees," their leader said in Spanish. All of them were heavily armed.

"Kneel, Jeff," I said.

"Hands clasped behind your heads."

We waited while they discussed us among themselves.

"Rise." They cuffed our hands behind our backs and then searched us roughly.

"I wish to see the American ambassador," I said in Spanish.

They laughed and fast-marched us up the balance of the hill and into a big van, army insignia on the side. For the next ten minutes it was all I could do to try to get my breathing back to normal, the bumpy ride not helping as we sat on narrow benches in the back, Jeff's right leg now manacled to my left.

"You all right?" Jeff asked.

"Fine. Terrific."

"We're in trouble."

"Not if you keep quiet. None of this CSIS stuff, OK?"

"What are you planning to tell them?" he asked.

"Enough to win their sympathy. Just let me think for a while."

I didn't really need to think about my story line. There was only one I could follow. Admittedly, I should have seen the dangerous direction my thinking was taking. I should have understood the anger that was moving to front row center, ready to leap up on the stage.

"Ben?"

"What?"

"You looked like you'd passed out. You were sitting there with your eyes screwed shut."

"I'm fine."

"You're sick. They should be taking you to a doctor."

"Don't make me laugh." I coughed again, nothing coming up. Pain in my chest. After a while I found myself leaning against him, my head tipped against his shoulder, and I pulled away.

"How long…" I said.

"About twenty minutes. I used the time to pray."

"Pray for both of us," I said, coughing again. "I don't have the strength."

"You had enough strength to dream of killing Harry Simpson."

"Why? What did I say?"

"Nothing intelligent. But I heard the words 'kill Harry' at least a couple of times. I thought your dreams would be more creative."

"It's not time for cre—" The coughing started again, and I had to bend forward.

Five minutes later we took a sharp turn and stopped. The back doors opened and soldiers dragged us out into a dusty street, ramshackle cement buildings on both sides, some sort of guardhouse with white peeling paint right in front. A crowd gathered but kept its distance.

"He's sick," Jeff said. "Needs doctor."

"What?" a soldier asked.

"Sick," pointing at me.

"I have a fever," I said in Spanish. "Doctor." That netted me a clout on the side of the head and Jeff a kick in the knee that put him on the ground.

"Come this way." This from a large man who'd just come out of the guardhouse. He wore some ridiculous dress uniform, sky blue with a red sash. Maybe somebody had warned him company was coming.

Jeff got up, pain on his face, and the guy in the clown suit led us into his office—big, opulent, bad taste reeking from everywhere. I couldn't stop coughing.

"Sit."

We sat on wooden chairs, side by side.

"Who are you and why did you enter our country illegally?"

"My name—" I said, then the coughing started again.

"His name is Ben Sylvester. I'm Jeff Mancuso. We were kidnapped in Canada by the rebel Hector who was killed last night at the border by the Juanitan army. We escaped. There was no other means to enter your country and our lives were at risk in Juanita."

"What did he say?" asked the commandant.

I groaned and asked for a pen and wrote it all down in Spanish and signed it and made Jeff sign it too.

"Hector is dead?"

"Yes, we assume so," I said.

"Were you with him?"

"He sent us down a trail to the river. I think he knew there was a battle waiting for him." The coughing had settled down for a moment.

"A brave man. We had hoped for great things from him."

"Why? What does he have to do with your country?"

"That is none of your affair."

"There's more," I said, before I went into another fit, feeling myself weakening by the minute. "There was a spy in Hector's camp. The man who sold Hector the guns also worked for the president of Juanita. We were supposed to be found dead with the rebels so the president could tell everyone that the Americans were supporting the revolutionaries."

"This man who sold the guns," the commandant said.

"A bad man," I said. "Very…" Everything was looking hazy to me now, like an autumn fog, but I felt unusually comfortable. It was very warm, a great softness enveloping the room.

Waking slowly, my mind rising to the surface, eyes forming slits to block the sudden appearance of bright light. I was afraid.

A different room, someone in a green smock standing over me. I was lying on a sofa, feet and head propped up by its arms. Fancy room in American style, light coming from the windows and the flashlight in the man's hand. I pulled back, reached for the top of the sofa.

"Take it easy, Ben." American voice. "You've been very sick, but you're safe now. This is the U.S. embassy."

"Who are you?"

"Jake Davidson. I run a clinic in town here. You'll be all right in a couple of days. Looks like a jungle fever of some kind plus a cold."

"What kind of jungle fever?"

"Probably just malaria. Someone broke into our lab last week and wrecked it after stealing us blind, so I can't do any official tests. As far as I can see, your lung congestion is contributing to your weakness. We'll start you on antibiotics and see how you do. The fever should blow through in a few days."

"Jeff?"

"In a waiting room nearby. You only got here an hour ago. Get some sleep."

"Yes."

"We've been trying to reach your wife. Mr. Mancuso said she was out of town."

"Yes. Can't reach her." I drifted off.

Sixteen hours later, or so they told me, I woke up and the fever was down to a dull roar. My chest still ached, but my head felt clear.

Outside the room I heard a low voice, chock full of authority, saying, "So you'll call me the second he's awake?"

Someone answered him.

"I'm awake," I said, but my voice was shot and I couldn't even manage a decent croak. On the table next to my bed was a bell. I grabbed it and shook it. Whoever it was wanted answers, and I was hoping like crazy he hadn't already questioned Jeff.

The doctor got into the room first, checked me over, then abandoned me to a hard looking man in a black suit.

"You're a heavy sleeper," he said.

"I've been sick."

"You've been busy. Why don't you tell me the whole story?" He sat down on the plastic chair to my right, the window so bright behind him that looking at him made my eyes water.

I told him everything except Jeff's background and the plan my fevered mind had been hatching before I'd passed out. When I was done, he stared at me, weighing something.

"Mr. Sylvester, I'm going to tell you two versions of what's happening back in the States even while I speak."

"Go ahead," I said, feeling exhausted again.

"Version one: A certain Harry Simpson has accused you to the FBI of running illegal arms to the rebels of Juanita."

"Well, that confirms one thing for me," I said, trying to mask the panic.

"Which is?"

"I'm out of a job. My boss hates me."

"Version two," he went on. "You and Mancuso were kidnapped. We've got our own video—sound and picture—of you being snatched at Harrison Lake. And we've got enough data to link Simpson to the arms."

"So arrest him," I said. "Arrest the whole company. I'm sure they're supporting him. You know I'm innocent. And Jeff—"

"Works for CSIS." Ouch.

"So you're telling me that you watched us get snatched and didn't even try to bail us out?"

"Not me."

"Others of your ilk. Why?"

"Our trail from Simpson to the arms wasn't strong enough for a jury. We were hoping with you involved that Simpson would show his hand. When the rebels snatched you, we figured they had some purpose for you, and we were sure Simpson would give further instructions or maybe even go to Juanita himself."

"Instead," I said, "he kept himself chummy with the president of Juanita and ignored the rebels so he could complete his plan to leave Jeff and me dead along with Hector and his men."

"We couldn't have known or we would have stopped it." An apology?

"When the big guy met me at Harrison Lake, did you know what he was planning?"

"No."

"So he could have killed me on the spot and you would have just watched."

"I wasn't responsible for that part of the mission."

"Oh, I'm so sorry. Far be it from me—"

"Mr. Sylvester, where are your wife and kids?"

"Safe. Have you got out an A.P.B. on them?"

"No."

"So you don't have enough evidence for arrests?"

"Simpson and his company are very smooth."

"I guess I'll just have to lay low then until you nail them."

"Do that," he said.

My hands were shaking so hard, I was glad I'd kept them under the covers.

CHAPTER THIRTEEN

A week later, Jeff and I flew into Calgary, Canada, under assumed names. Our passports were perfect because they'd been issued by the U.S. government. Until the feds tightened their noose around Libertec—fat chance of that—they wanted us out of the way. At least that's the story I was told.

Our CIA contact in Central America had ordered the two of us to take a cab to a safe house in the southeast area of Calgary and stay put. Someone would deliver us groceries and videos. If I planned to call Karen, I should use a pay phone at the airport. I didn't.

They were so smug about it, making sure we'd have no trouble from officials when we landed, giving us each five hundred in cash just in case. Within half a mile in the cab, we'd figured out their elaborate tailing procedure put on to make sure we reached the safe house safely. But we had no intention of staying in official custody.

There was a big mall on the way, perfect for our purposes, and we got the cabby to drop us there. For a few minutes we moved fast through the crowds of shoppers, then we split up, Jeff passing me most of his $500 just before he darted into a department store.

I walked into a bookstore and ducked through the staff area in the back out into a maze of concrete back corridors. Once I'd found an outside door behind the mall, I walked several blocks in the late summer heat, then took a city bus to another part of the city, maxed out my daily cash allowance at a bank machine, rented a third-rate car, and drove to the city of Red Deer where I left the car a block from the local branch of the same rental company.

Caught a Greyhound to Edmonton. Took local transit across the city, found a pay phone and called Jeff's brother Dave in Mission, B.C. Edith Mancuso, Dave's wife, answered. When she heard my voice, there was a confused flurry, silence, then one word, "Ben?" Karen's voice sounded so tiny, vulnerable.

"Yes."

"Ben? Is that you?"

"It's me. I'm OK."

"Where? Oh Lord, we thought you were—"

"I'm fine. Jeff too. We're not far away, and I hope I can get to you in two or three days."

"What happened? Where did you..." Stronger now. "Dave came and told us you'd vanished and we were in danger."

"Did anyone follow you to Canada?"

"No. Not that we could see."

"They'll have traced the border records. They know you're in Canada."

"It's a big country. We'll be careful."

"Do that."

"What's happening, Ben? Can't you tell me someth—"

"I'll tell you soon. Just stay low till I get there. I love you."

"But what—"

I hung up.

Found a cheap motel, paid cash in advance, false name. Took a cab next morning to a nearby town, bought a Greyhound to Prince George in British Columbia, still four hundred miles from Karen. Picked up some secondhand clothes and hitchhiked to Vancouver with a nice couple who offered to buy all my meals. They seemed lonely, but I didn't talk much. I paid for my own meals.

They left me on Broadway in Vancouver, and I found a travel agent who had just what I wanted. Made a call to a grand old lady who agreed to everything, though she was baffled. Told her where to find the place I needed to corner Harry.

I took the West Coast Express commuter train to Mission, about seventy miles to the east, late that afternoon. Quick cab ride to Dave Mancuso's house.

Karen greeted me with a deluge of tears while Jack and Jimmie mostly screamed. We all hugged, and emotions ran riot. There was something so powerful about it, so beyond what I could have explained even a few years before. Gradually the chaos died down, and Karen and I could look at each other. I'd never noticed the gray in her hair, the lines that marked every tribulation that had hit us since Simpson started sabotaging our lives.

"What happened to you?" she said. "I have to know."

"Not here. Let's sit down," I said, moving toward the living room.

"Can I get you anything?" Edith Mancuso asked as she came out of the kitchen.

"Nothing, thanks. Kids?" They shook their heads. "Has Jeff arrived yet?"

"No. He called and said he'd be here tomorrow."

Dave Mancuso was in the living room, and I shook his hand.

"Thank you for bailing out my family."

"Glad to help."

We sat down, and I went through the whole thing, from Harrison Lake to the present. When I finished an hour later, I was exhausted, as if someone were stealing my air, as if I were being consumed.

"Ben?" Karen's voice coming out of an auditory fog. "You're shaking."

"Trace of fever."

"You'll be all right now. You're safe."

I looked at her, at Dave and Edith next to her, the kids on the floor, and wondered how to break the next part, even wondered for half a second whether I had the right to do what I planned. Should I have told her privately later? Maybe, but I felt this needed to be a communal decision if only to quiet my own doubts about it.

"None of us are safe," I said.

"Surely the authorities—" Dave said.

"The authorities photographed Jeff and me being kidnapped. They sacrificed us in the hope that Simpson might give himself away."

"Harry can't reach us here," Karen said. "You're scaring the children." Actually, Jimmie was squirming, showing boredom. Jack was the one staring at me, his eyes like bottomless pits.

"We have to deal with reality," I said. "Harry's working under the orders of Libertec. The whole organization's rotten. But they don't know how much the FBI knows about them. All they can see is that I got away from Juanita alive."

"You came into Canada under tight security," Dave broke in. "With all the flimflam of the past few days, no one could possibly know where you are."

"The FBI and CSIS don't have enough evidence to nail Simpson, let alone Libertec. If the feds show their hand now to protect us, they'll blow the investigation and Simpson will find us, count on it."

"No," Karen said. "Not again."

"What?"

"I know you, Ben. You're not going after Libertec yourself."

"Not by myself. Jeff's helping." The room was too cold. I could feel shivers hovering near my spine.

"You lost your mind?" Dave said.

"Listen to my idea first."

"No," Karen said. "Look at you—you're shaking all over."

"I've got a plan, a good one."

"Me too," Karen said. "Bed. Right now. And you'd better sleep till noon or—"

"Or what?"

"I don't know or what. Please, just get some sleep."

Too beat to protest, I let them bundle me off to bed. For a while I wallowed in the quiet, the false assurance that all was safe and warm. Banish the terrors of the night, all is peace, drifting, waking again, calm yourself, sleep.

Then Harry Simpson made a mistake, and I threw him, and he fell hard and I jumped on him and started doing unspeakable things to his body while he pleaded with me to stop, to have some measure of mercy. But mercy and Harry were oil and water and I—

The sound of Jimmie whooping past the bedroom door dashed the death-plot I'd been hatching, and I rolled on my back and stared at the blue of the sky sneaking in around a corner of the curtain. Karen was up already. The clock radio said 10:47. I'd slept all night.

"You saw how much I enjoyed it," I said to God while I lay there on my back. "The dream. What I did to Harry."

Could I sense divine disapproval? Surprise?

"It's clear to me," I said, "that you were with me every second when I was down in Juanita, almighty God that you are. It was more than just sickness that let me see the angels. You were trying to take me past the fear, weren't you?"

But the scene my dream had woven in my mind was so B-movie that it embarrassed me. Picture this:

They took him against his will and beat him and tried to kill him. Now he's back and he knows the only way to regain his manhood is to fight them where they live.

"That's not me, all right?" I said. "I'm grateful to be here alive, but I'm not all set to live out *Death Wish XVII*. The only reason I'm taking him on is that he's going to kill us if I don't. It has nothing to do with vengeance."

I sensed no answer. Slowly I got up and put on my borrowed robe.

Karen was in the kitchen drinking coffee. "What are you doing up? It's too early."

"I'm all right. Really. Getting better." I grabbed an orange from a bowl, ate it, took my antibiotic capsule.

"Jimmie's so noisy," she said.

"It's OK. There were times over these past few weeks that I would've given anything to hear his noise. Any sign of Jeff?"

"No."

"Where are Dave and Edith?"

"Groceries."

"The kids?"

"Watching a video in the den."

"I guess we need to talk."

She got up, poured me coffee, looked me in the face. "You have to call them, Ben. The police, whoever. Tell them where we are and ask for protection."

"Won't work."

"If Harry and Libertec knew they were being watched by the FBI, they'd never come after us. They'd probably try to flee the country."

"These people, Karen," I said. "You have to understand that they won't just fade away. They've been operating for decades and they're going to hang on even if it means eliminating their enemies."

"Let someone else catch them. We have to make a new life for ourselves."

"I'm planning to go ahead no matter what," I said. "Jeff and I have a plan."

"What, to get yourselves killed?"

"Nobody's going to die. At least listen to me."

It took me ten minutes to go over it with her point by point, answering her many objections. There wasn't any way I could convince her that this was the only course open to us. I could hardly convince myself, but I wanted her to understand that this wasn't just some stupid stunt to get one up on Harry Simpson.

"Can I say anything to change your mind?" she said finally.

"No. I'm just going to draw him out, force him to talk. He'll have to understand that hurting me won't save him."

"What if I called the police myself?"

"Go ahead. There's the phone."

"Do you have to be so cold about it?" There were tears on her cheeks.

"This thing is for keeps and there isn't any room for softness."

"Not even for me?"

"Of course for you. Not for them."

"Are you planning to kill Harry when you're done with him?"

I spilled my coffee. "What are you talking about?" I said, throwing a dishcloth on the mess.

"How much do you hate him, Ben?" She hadn't moved, her arm propping up her cup, her body leaning forward. "How much?"

"Hate doesn't enter into it."

"I know you, Ben. I can see right into your very soul."

"What do you see?"

"A man who was terrorized and humiliated, who watched a good man be betrayed and killed, and now you've got to do the macho thing and punish the one who's responsible."

"That's not who I am. This is to save our lives. These people are going to kill us."

"Let someone else stop them, someone who can protect us."

"Who? You of all people should want me to pound Harry into the dirt," I said.

"Why? Because of what he did? Because he made me angry at God?"

"Yes."

"I found out while you were gone, Ben..." She paused. "There isn't room for anger if you want to go on living."

"You were seething with it before I got snatched. People don't just abandon the kind of baggage you were carrying."

She turned her head and stared out the window. "About three or four nights after you disappeared, after Dave had brought us here, I...this sounds so...I had a dream. You and I were walking along a road in the dark. It was foggy. And you were telling me that one day I'd stop fighting God and the only thing that would be left was love. It was so peaceful."

"I know. We walked. The fog made it hard to see more than a few steps."

She turned back to me with surprise. "Then suddenly something or someone just snatched you away, and I screamed. But a voice came out of the fog and said, 'Trust me,' over and over. I'd never heard anything so...do you understand, Ben? He was there. He's always been there, even when we couldn't see him. Even the horror in Africa."

"I know."

"So I said to him, 'Send angels to Ben to watch over him.'"

"I saw them."

"What?"

"In Juanita, when we were fleeing from the army, I swear I saw angels."

Her face turned hard then. I wasn't ready for it. "I won't let you destroy everything by going after Harry Simpson."

I reached for her hand, and she didn't pull away. "It's too late, Karen."

"Why?"

"The plan's already running. We can't stop it now."

e'd been waiting for two days in Harrison, and the tension was showing around his eyes when we met at the rockery by the beach, the little man-made waterfalls and pools choked with coins from the summer make-a-wish crowd.

He'd lost me for a while after the massacre in Juanita. Now if he wanted to find me and learn how much I could damage him, he had to meet me on my terms. Of course, he'd also be looking for ways to do me in if it suited his purposes. I could almost feel his bloodlust.

"Glad you could come, Harry," I said. "Did you bring my paycheck?"

He handed it over, saying nothing.

"I think I'll cash this one fast," I said. "You guys better not stop payment."

"If you're through with the clown act," he said, "maybe we could get down to something important."

"You probably want someplace secure so we can really talk, heart to heart. We'll pick up the key at that shop over there. I found a very out of the way place for us. You'll love it."

"We could deal with everything here."

"And risk being overheard or me getting wasted in a drive-by shooting? Come on, Harry."

I walked over to the shop, Simpson following, and got the key. Simpson made a point of asking the guy if I'd been to the place in advance and seemed reassured to hear I hadn't.

I drove the car I'd brought with me, heading up the west side of Harrison Lake, Simpson doing a glum passenger routine despite the view revealed by the late summer morning sun. I didn't know why I'd chosen Harrison Lake for the meeting except that it gave me perverse pleasure to bring Harry back to the scene of the crime.

The road turned to gravel and rose high above the lake, giving the occasional fabulous sighting of the water and islands below. About three miles along, I pulled into a side bay and got out of the car.

"What?" Harry said.

I stared at the sky in all directions. No sign of a chopper. The road behind was empty. Below was Echo Island where Hector's people had snatched Jeff and me.

"Just checking," I said, getting back into the car. He grunted.

The car was a rental, and I punished it along the road, wanting to get there, get it done. Lamb to the slaughter, Harry. How does it feel?

Twenty kilometers, the guy had said. Twelve miles. Then a side road for two more. Can't miss it. No power, wood stove if we needed it.

The route was easy to follow, and we ran into no trouble on the way. I pulled the car right in front of the cabin and got out. Opened the trunk and took out a briefcase.

The place was as rustic as I'd expected it to be—a big rough-hewn table in the middle, wooden chairs, bunks on both sides, wood stove in the back with cupboards next to it and a built-in basin. Washroom in the left corner. Running water, the guy had said. Piped down right out of a stream.

I put the briefcase on the table and flicked it open, Simpson trying to peer over my shoulder.

"Back off," I said. He sat down on one of the chairs on the other side of the table, his face showing nothing.

"Here's the situation, Harry," I said a few minutes later, after I'd looked over everything once more. "I don't want to have to watch for snipers anymore. Or listen to things that go bump in the night."

"Then go live in Acapulco and keep your mouth shut."

"If that was the right answer, you wouldn't be here."

"Show me what you've got."

"You know, Harry," I said, "your meek-as-a-lamb routine is really becoming to you. You should do it more often."

"Only a fool starts blazing away before he knows what he's facing."

"Before I show you, I want you to remember that these are only copies. The originals are elsewhere."

"I'm not stupid. Show me what you've got."

I gave it to him one piece at a time:

- photo of Harry meeting with the spy in my mother-in-law's company
- forty-page statement from me about every dirty deed of his that I was aware of, from the knife wound I'd taken in the arm to Saluso to Juanita, all of it connected back to Simpson
- a signed statement from Hector saying that Harry Simpson was the man who arranged to sell him the armaments.

"How did you get that?" Harry said. He'd lost his bureaucratic vocabulary, I noticed.

"When poor Hector realized his movement had been betrayed by a spy, he was eager to write it for me. I didn't even have to ask."

"OK." Harry got up. "Nothing goes any further until I check out you and this place. First you."

Stripping down to underwear was getting tedious, but I didn't want him clamming up on me. He found no wires on me, then went over the whole cabin.

"I've never been here," I said.

"Someone else might have been."

When he was done, he sat down again, picked up Hector's statement about buying the guns.

"This is a lie," he said. "Or someone told him who I was. We met in Juanita, but I never told him my name."

"I'm sure he had ways. You admit you sold him the guns?"

"I admit nothing, Ben. Let's cut down to the bottom line and you can tell me what you want."

"The first thing I want is for you to listen to me. The second is for you and Libertec to back off us."

"On the basis of this?" He tossed Hector's statement back into the briefcase.

My cell phone went off, and I dug it out from under Hector's statement.

Jeff was on the other end. "Two guys came up in a pickup. Told me they were going to fish, but what do you know, they forgot their poles."

I glared at Simpson but spoke into the phone. "So what did you tell them?"

"That if they left really quick, I might pretend I hadn't seen them. They turned around."

"Don't take chances like that. You were just supposed to observe."

"I thought you needed some time."

"I do and I'm grateful."

"Don't be too grateful. I'm sure they'll be back."

I hung up.

"Harry," I said, throwing the phone back into the briefcase, "I told you to come alone."

"They're just a bit of muscle. How was I to know you didn't bring me up here to do me in?"

"Your muscle's run out on you, so do what you're told."

"Which is?"

"Shut up and listen."

"If this is going to be some crybaby lecture about all the ways I've done you wrong, why don't you save it."

I reached back into the briefcase, grabbed the phone, dialed. "Jeff?" I said. "This isn't working. Call Dave and tell him to release the stuff to the Mounties."

"No," Simpson said.

I stared at Simpson long and hard.

"OK, Jeff, hold off for a while. I'll call you."

"Who else knows about this?" Simpson said.

"Three of us."

"You had a lecture to deliver."

"Man named Hector," I said.

"Just another pathetic little revolutionary."

"Let me guess," I said. "When I came back from Juanita the first time and told you Hector's people had rescued me, you went down there and suggested to Hector that the only way to win in Juanita was to fight."

"Save it, Ben. You've got your briefcase full of bad news. Let's just cut our deal and get back to civilization."

"I'm calling the shots. We're going to discuss this." He looked at the wall above my head. "So you convinced Hector that a fair election was never going to happen and arranged to sell him a shipload of weapons. Where'd Hector get the funds in such a hurry?"

"Who knows? Probably a bunch of bleeding heart fans from the U.S."

"Doesn't matter. You made the deal, then you went to the president of Juanita and sold Hector to him. At first I thought that was Libertec's idea, but now I suspect you thought up that part all on your own."

"I—"

"Shut up, Harry. The president hung a big threat over one of Hector's men and got the guy to turn over all the data he needed to wipe out the revolution before it could get off the ground."

I couldn't stand being across the table from him, so I got up, walked a few steps and leaned back against a window sill. "But the president had a problem," I went on. "The U.S. was pressuring him for a free election. If he wiped out Hector, the PR would be very nasty. Sure, he could play golden boy, let Hector organize a legitimate opposition party, and then hold a real election. But the president feared he'd lose."

"It's getting kind of convoluted, Ben."

"So you arranged for Hector's people to kidnap me so my American body would be found among the dead revolutionaries and imported armaments, a body that could be linked to the CIA if you dropped enough evidence around. The only reason it got fouled up is that Hector became suspicious of his second in command and hid the guns outside the camp."

I walked toward the table. "Why me?" I said. "Could it have been that you suspected I might be ready to blow the whistle on you? Go ahead, Harry. I'll let you talk now."

"This is all so simple for you, isn't it," he said. "What a smart guy you are to have figured everything out so well. I'll have to give you a C+."

"Not an A?"

"To get an A you'd have to grasp all the nuances. Your explanation has no creativity to it."

"What's missing?"

"What's missing is the fact that goody two-shoes doesn't cut it in a world where the tough guys make up the rules. We started out naive, but Libertec grew up."

"Into what—a front for gunrunning and revolution?"

"Into what it takes to really help."

"Is that why you sold guns to Hector, then betrayed him to his president?"

"That's your story. Believe what you want."

"Are you ready to deal with me?"

"Let's hear the offer." He stared, his emotions unreadable.

"My evidence," I said, "will go into a safe place. Two other people, or maybe a few more, will know everything. If I or my family are attacked by you people, the evidence goes to the FBI."

"How original," he said. "I think I saw the same plot on the late show last night in my hotel room. So what happens if one of you has an accident that has nothing to do with me?"

"Pray that we don't, Harry."

"Seems to me you've got diddly here. Our people might decide to back off you because you're such a nuisance when you're riled. But don't go getting all superior."

"Hector deserved better than he got."

"Being a crybaby won't bring him back. He dared and he lost. Big deal."

"He was a good man, and he might have accomplished something if you idiots hadn't talked him into buying guns."

"You helped him too. You worked on his propaganda for him even though you knew he had guns."

"How would you know that, Harry?"

"People tell me things. I think I have a gift for listening."

"All I did was help him get into what he should have been doing instead of arming hims—"

"You don't have to justify yourself to me." He got up. "I'm tired of life in the big woods. Take me back."

"You'll call the dogs off?"

"What dogs are those?"

"The ones that are bound to come looking for me or my family now that I know what I know."

"Sure. I'll call them off."

I didn't believe a word of it, but the plan was to get him talking, not to trust his assurances.

"How close was I to the truth about Hector?" I asked.

"Dead on, Ben. Take me back."

The phone rang and I picked it up. A sound like gasping. "Get out, Ben. Now!"

"Who?"

"Big…" Gasping. "Ugly pickup. Get out!"

I slammed the briefcase shut over the evidence, grabbed the handle, bolted for the back door. Simpson cut me off, and I swung the case and caught him on the side of the head, climbed over him as he fell, ran through the door, up the hill, stumbling around trees and scrub, my crummy leg messing up my speed.

A hundred feet up the slope, I turned. No one was behind

me. I hadn't hit Harry that hard. He must have been waiting for the goons to arrive. Dust in the distance—a vehicle moving up fast. I climbed higher.

Pickup truck in front of the cabin. Two men. Rifles. I only hoped Jeff hadn't taken too much of a chance. We'd rehearsed it all except for Jeff stopping the truck that first time.

The men came out the back door fast, eyes searching for me, rifles at their shoulders.

"Ben!" Jeff's voice, above me, to my right. I couldn't see him because there was a big rock on the slope between us. Carefully, using scrub as a screen, I crawled behind the rock.

A bullet tore through the branches of a fir tree to my right as I got up and moved through the brush to my left toward Jeff. I risked a look down the slope and saw Simpson grab a rifle from one of his men and start firing all over the slope. The other guy joined in and the branches around me started ripping off in little bursts of fury.

They were moving fast now, below me and to my left, then Jeff was there grabbing my arm, and the firing stopped as they realized they'd have to climb to find us. I heard them thrashing in the dense brush but we were moving out of range, heading sideways on the slope, then down. A few minutes later we spotted Jeff's car where he'd left it on a side trail.

It started noisily, and we spattered dirt all over the trees as we tore out of there, Simpson and his men firing in our direction, shooting blind, too far away to reach us. But I knew they were running for their truck.

CHAPTER FIFTEEN

About the time they started shooting at us from their speeding pickup, I realized what a desperately foolish plan this was, pure Ben Sylvester from the old days. Only I had Jeff with me now, and I remembered the last time I'd dragged him into danger in Canada. Once again we were about to die and he hadn't even fouled up this time.

We'd made a clean getaway from the cabin and traveled for about five minutes, when I looked back and saw the pickup about a mile behind us, dust rising high, before we took a sharp turn and sped up a hill.

"They're following," I told Jeff. "Push it harder."

"Don't sweat it."

"Maybe you should let me drive. I'm faster."

He snorted. "I'm crazier. No one nuttier than Jeff Mancuso." He put us into a four-wheel drift around the corner, forcing the car straight a second before we went over the bank.

On the straightaway that followed, I looked back again. They were closer. Jeff moved the speed up a few more notches and for a moment the pickup faded, then it put on its own burst.

Something wanged into the back of the car. One of Harry's goons was leaning out of a passenger window, and I saw a rifle barrel.

"Weave!" I shouted. They were no more than fifty yards away now and closing fast.

"Think of something, Einstein!" Jeff shouted.

"Like what?"

Then just ahead, coming toward us, was a Chrysler van, some family out for a day of wilderness, probably expecting nothing more exciting than a distant bear sighting. The pickup hit its brakes and widened the gap. Jeff let the van pass, then put our car into a sharp 180 slide and came up right behind it, heading back in the direction of the cabin.

The pickup swung around too, then hesitated, came to a stop. Out the back window, I watched it gradually drop out of my vision.

"They'll just wait till we drive out of here and then ambush us," I said.

"No they won't." Jeff grinned at me like a boy scout with a new badge. "We have cell phones." He slowed to let the family in the van get far ahead of us.

"Who you gonna call, Jeff?"

"My contact." He pulled over, phoned someone and explained our situation. "One hour," he said to me when he was done.

"How do you know Simpson isn't going to come back up here and take us out before then? An hour's a long time."

"Let's go back to the cabin. We can hide the car, pick up the tapes, and then wait in the bush." He called his contact again to make the arrangements.

We drove fast, finally overtaking the van that was still moving at family speed. Near the cabin we put the car up a narrow side track where it could be found only if you left the road.

I'd checked with Karen's mother that morning on the location of the cameras in the cabin. They were so well masked that I wouldn't have seen them from a foot away if I didn't know they were there. Struggling to remember my instructions, we got the videos out. The cameras would have to be left behind.

"You think we got Simpson on film shooting at you?" Jeff asked.

"Probably."

"So why no elation?"

"He'll soon be up here again looking for us. Before the cops arrive. You tend to underestimate the problems."

"And you worry too much. All we have to do is hide in the woods."

"Let's go then." For the past half hour I'd been feeling very warm, with an occasional chill. I told myself to hang on, but I knew the fever was lurking in the wings.

We climbed up the slope until my leg started barking at me, then found cover where we could watch the approach to the cabin. Sure enough, ten minutes later, Simpson and his two helpers showed up. They went inside, and I remembered too late that we'd left the table in a corner where I'd used it to stand on to get the last of the videos out.

There was a shout, then some thumping and tearing, then Simpson burst out the back door with a rifle and started shooting in all directions. Something whistled by twenty feet to our right, and we put our heads down.

The firing stopped, then Harry shouted, "I'll kill you, Ben." I felt it first in my legs, the trembling, then my arms. It wasn't all fever.

More gunfire, a few shots hitting even closer than the last

time, and I clasped my arms around my chest to stop the shaking.

"Take it easy, Ben," Jeff whispered. "The cops'll be here soon."

"How does Harry know we're up here?"

"It's me. While you were getting the last video, I wrote a note and threw it on the table. All it said was, 'Where are the cameras, Harry?' I thought he might stop trying to silence us if he knew we had hard evidence."

"We're dead," I told him.

"The cops will be here in ten minutes."

"You got guarantees?" I couldn't stop the shaking.

"It was too early for this, Ben. We should've waited until you were well."

"And given enough time for Harry to find us? Forget it."

Jeff took a look through the branches. "They're moving up the slope. A hundred yards to our left and maybe fifty down."

"Any ideas," I whispered, "or do you only specialize on getting people *into* situations?"

Actually there was a weird logic to what Jeff had done. The one bug in the plan had been how we'd inform Simpson that we had videotaped my meeting with him and its violent aftermath. Jeff had solved the problem for us, but hadn't given us room to get away.

"They'll be here soon, Ben. The cops said an hour. Hang on."

Easy for him to say. His teeth weren't banging together hard enough to chip them.

"Where's Simpson now?"

Jeff looked. "Just below us, coming this way."

"O God," I said, and it was the most genuine prayer I'd ever uttered. The whole thing had fallen apart and I wasn't sure I could run any more, let alone walk.

"Dust on the road, Ben."

Rifles firing again, branches snapping over our heads before moving off to our left. From the way they covered the whole slope, they must have had a sack of bullet clips with them.

"Cops, Ben. Two cars." The firing stopped. "Four guys are coming up the slope."

"Where's Simpson?"

"I don't know."

"Stay down. Let the cops find us."

"That's a good way to get shot." He stood up. "Over here," he said, loud enough to startle deer in the next valley. "We're not armed. Watch out for the guys with rifles to the north of us."

The cops reached us easily, RCMP in uniform. No sign of Simpson. Twenty minutes later, after they'd half dragged me down the hill because my leg had swollen and I was shaking too hard to breathe right, the cops had us back in the cabin. Two stayed with us while the other two went to look for signs of Simpson.

In twenty minutes the searchers came back. "Nothing," one of them said.

"How hard did you try?" Jeff asked.

"Don't give us trouble." He sat on a chair, breathing hoarsely. "By the time we get dogs up here, they'll be too far away to matter."

"Except to me," I said. "They're going to kill me."

The shaking had stopped, but I was feeling very warm again.

"We need you safe first, Mr. Sylvester, then we can deal with Mr. Simpson. In your case, I'd say our first stop will be a hospital. And CSIS wants to talk to Jeff here."

They put us in a car and I remember a blur of trees and dust and glimpses of a lake. A sensation that I was watching myself while nausea hovered in the wings. The day had started with such promise, because I knew I was in control. But you can't control everything for sure, you fool. I thought you'd learned that when Saluso shot you in the leg.

I remember watching myself and praying, begging God to stop me always being a bull in a china shop, grinning savagely at the cliché. Wondering how much I hated Simpson, knowing it was dangerous because I needed a cold rational mind. Hating him because he'd turned me into a quivering lump of fear yet once again.

And that was when I understood that Karen was right. This wasn't just a wild bid to win insurance for ourselves. I wanted Simpson dead.

I woke up in yet another hospital bed with a nurse staring into my face. Fog lifted gradually while I nurtured frustration. I felt suddenly sick, and the nurse saw the look on my face and held out a bag and helped me until I emptied my stomach and she wiped my face with a cloth.

"Doctor," I croaked. "I have to find out what—"

"He'll be here in a minute. You'll be all right."

"Where?"

"Chilliwack." I pictured a city south of Harrison and Agassiz. "They brought you in from Harrison. This is a hospital."

"Where's Jeff?"

"Who?"

"Where are the people, the ones who brought me in here?"

"I have no idea. You do have a police officer outside the door though."

"Bring him."

She brought him in, awkward in his obviously new uniform, scrubbed baby face.

"The people who brought me…"

"They left. Said they'd be back in a couple of hours. Do you want me to call them?" He flipped open a cell phone.

"No. You need to take me…" I lost my words then, fog coming back as I tried to get out of bed.

"What are you doing?" Voice of authority. Doctor. "Get back in bed." The cop scooted back out the door. "Nurse, this isn't a circus. Are you charging admission?"

"Sorry." She left too.

"Mr. Sylvester, the reason you're here is that you've avoided medical attention. Don't compound the problem."

"What've I got?"

"One of those new strains of malaria. Did you use antimalarials when you were in the tropics?"

"No. I didn't have much of a chance to get ready for the trip." My mind was clearer again, I thought.

"Didn't anyone treat you?"

"Doctor at the embassy down there. The fever went down."

"He didn't tell you what you had?"

"There was no way to test for it. He gave me antibiotics for my chest infection."

"We've started you on treatment, and you'll be taking lots of pills, but it will have to be monitored. Malaria these days can get pretty nasty."

"I have to talk to Jeff."

He frowned. "I really don't want to know what all the cloak and dagger is about. If you're planning to leave anytime soon, forget it."

"I don't feel safe."

"Work that out with the cop. Just make sure you stay put." He must have slept through bedside manner in medical school.

Two hours later I heard Jeff's voice out in the hall. My mind was clearer still and I was ready for good news.

But his face told another story. "This has gotten messy, Ben."

"Did you play them the videos?"

"I did. Picture and sound came out perfectly—Simpson admitting to the gunrunning and to shafting Hector. Even a good view of Simpson shooting at us."

"So it's over."

"No. They took the tapes."

"You were supposed to make copies."

"No time, Ben. They wouldn't have allowed it anyway."

"When are they going to arrest Simpson?"

"That's the complicated part. They're not."

CHAPTER SIXTEEN

W e thought of pulling some sort of Laurel and Hardy routine to get me out, but even to us it sounded ridiculous. The cop was supposed to be guarding me from Simpson, but he also made a very effective jail-keeper.

Jeff had explained to me what happened at his meeting. CSIS hadn't let him copy the videos we'd made, nor had they given them back. When Jeff described Simpson's attack on us, they got uncomfortable and told him there wouldn't be an A.P.B. on Harry as long as Libertec was under investigation.

"But Simpson's trying to kill us," Jeff had protested.

All they would offer was protection.

I'd be in the hospital for a couple more days of medication, then I'd be released as long as I agreed to take the rest of my pills faithfully and check in with a clinic in a week or whenever I felt symptoms, whichever came first. No one had told Jeff how they'd guard me once I was out on the street.

The whole thing had been botched. Our little plan had come unglued, and all we'd done was antagonize Simpson. It had been such a simple scheme—arrange for Karen's mom, through her electronics company, to hide video cameras with sound in the cabin; lure Simpson there and get him talking, then force him to act against me while I escaped out the back door. The thing we'd missed was how hard it would be to lose Simpson on the chase back to town.

I motioned to Jeff to close the door. "They can't protect us," I told him. "Simpson is going to come after us because he doesn't know whether or not we still have the tapes."

"I tried like crazy to find out why nobody was going after him. They're hiding something." Yet there was something in Jeff's tone that told me he wasn't revealing all himself.

"What's been your relationship with CSIS? They give you a title or a job description when they hired you?"

"Nothing like that. All they gave me was a job at Electar and extra pay for watching their suspected spy."

"No special training?"

"They let me have a little camera. Taught me how to use it."

"Just silly stuff, then. So why you? Why not one of their own people?"

"Search me. I guess they thought I was pretty motivated to find out who was responsible for the things that had happened."

"But they've known about Simpson and his dirty deals for a couple of years now."

"They told me they needed more evidence before they could nail him."

"You gave them a photo of Harry meeting the spy at Electar. And we gave them videos of him admitting he sold guns to Hector. We even have footage of him shooting at us."

"They didn't seem to care."

"Maybe they've thought of a better way to take him out than arresting him."

"That kind of stuff doesn't work anymore," Jeff said. "CSIS has so many regulations that an agent can't even spit into the wind, let alone carry out a hit. Same for the Americans."

"I bet Libertec is worrying that they've got a loose cannon on their hands," I said.

"Who? Simpson?"

"Maybe CSIS or the CIA took notice when Hector got killed—"

"And told Libertec Harry was becoming a danger?"

"What if Libertec was doing all kinds of deals but carefully, never coming close to getting caught? Then Simpson, their point man, started getting greedy, doing a few side deals for himself. So the CIA told Libertec it was time to take Harry out."

"You do wild speculation really well, Ben. So why would the CIA talk to Libertec?"

"Because Libertec's been doing contract work for every government agency going. That's why they've never gotten caught. They do all the jobs the feds don't want on their own books."

"It doesn't work. You and I were kidnapped so our bodies could be left in the rebel camp to discredit the U.S. government. The CIA wouldn't have sanctioned something like that."

"That was probably all Simpson," I said. "No doubt he'd have a ready explanation for the Libertec bosses—probably something like the two of us planned our own disappearance so we could do a side deal with Hector."

"It's too much of a leap for me."

"Simpson needs to be taken out. If the cops and CSIS are backing off, they're letting someone else do it. My bet's on Libertec."

Jeff looked away.

"Is there something you want to tell me?" I asked. His face showed confusion, then a trace of that telltale shifty guilt I knew so well.

"All in all," he said, "the best place for you is right here with a guard outside. Let Libertec hunt Simpson down if they want him so bad."

"I thought you didn't buy my wild explanation."

"I do now."

"What are you hiding, Jeff?"

"Nothing."

"Right, and maybe this time one of your little secrets will get me killed."

"I'm trying to keep you alive. The way you blow up when I tell you things, it's a wonder I tell you anything. This time I don't want you blundering right into a bullet, OK?"

"At least help me get out of here."

"No. You're safer here."

"What's waiting for me out there other than Simpson?"

He got up and left the room without a word, and I knew for sure that his maddening habit of withholding information was really going to put me in the soup this time.

Some people assume there's a great gulf fixed between fight and flight, anger and fear. The truth is that they're more like blood brothers or maybe members of the same wrestling tag team. When one can't handle life, the other takes over.

The whole Juanita thing had scared the life out of me. The thought of Harry Simpson waiting for me out there or maybe planning a way to get to me in my hospital bed was enough to put me around the bend. But you can't live on fear. It doesn't feed you, it only saps your strength. And I could feel fear's tag team partner struggling to assert itself, to give me the courage to fight back.

What was more, I had a faith to rebuild because my trust level was in the minuses. It wasn't God's fault, it was mine for insisting on flying by the seat of my pants, too caught up in circumstance to reach for a safe haven. I'd hoped that God and I had settled things when Saluso's bullet plowed into my leg. But the struggle went on.

What I really wanted was to throttle Harry Simpson and regain something for myself. You want him dead, Ben. Say it.

"I want him dead," I said.

Will heaven smile on you if you bring Harry's scalp to God? Will he say, 'Well done, good and faithful servant. You have rid the world of one bad apple'?

Of course he won't, and I was still a good Christian family man who would never dream of living out any of my dark fantasies. People like Harry loved to gorge themselves on people like me because I could only dream about what I really wanted to do.

But maybe this time Harry would get a surprise. Maybe God would too.

Someone brought me lunch, and after that I tried to watch TV, but I caught myself feeding on the charge I got from some stupid revenge movie. About four, I shut it off and stared at the wall.

A sudden crash from somewhere not too far away, and I heard a curse, running feet. It took a few seconds to register, then I bolted to the door and confirmed that the cop was gone. I found myself moving to the closet, putting on my street clothes, starting to gasp with the effort, opening the door, heading down the hall away from the direction the cop had taken.

I rode the elevator to the ground floor and just walked out through the usual bustle of the hospital lobby. No wallet, of course, they store that for safekeeping, so there wasn't much point to what I'd done because I had no money to go anywhere.

"Ben." Jeff moved out from behind a bush in front of the hospital.

"I'm leaving whether you go with me or not," I said. "So make up your mind. We don't have much time."

"I've got a car down there." He looked agitated.

"Let's go."

We walked to it, the effort making me breathe hard. I realized I had no medication with me. Jeff drove us out of town, heading south.

"Where to?" he said.

"Anywhere that I don't compromise Karen and the kids."

"Back to the cabin?"

"Too obvious. Get to the freeway and head east." He did what I told him. Once we were moving at highway speed, I said to him, "Now tell me what you've been hiding."

"Nothing."

"Usually when you do this you have some twisted notion that it's better if I don't know. That's what your mind's probably buzzing with right now."

"Give me a break, Ben. You've escaped in spite of me warning you not to. Let's just find somewhere to hole up until we figure out the next step."

"You already know the next step, and lying to me is tarnishing your Christian testimony."

He banged on the steering wheel. "You really want to mess up your head? Just leave it alone and lay off me."

"I'll get it out of you, Jeff. I always do."

"And you'll win the prize for the biggest fool I ever met."

"You're the slickest. Tell me what's going on."

"It wasn't my fault. I didn't know until the day before we went up to the cabin."

"Spill it."

"Libertec isn't going after Simpson. Neither are the cops."

"So they're just going to let him go?"

"No."

"They've put a hit out on him? Hired the Mafia?"

"No."

"I swear, Jeff—"

"They've found somebody to kill Simpson for them. The poor schmuck doesn't even know."

"Who?"

He turned his head and looked at me.

"You."

I opened my mouth but nothing came out, so I closed it again, stared out the window at the flatland farms of the Fraser Valley, the mountains beyond to the east.

"I guess you'd better explain it," I said finally. "Everything from the beginning."

"I didn't know any of this, I swear. They got to me at the bus station in Vancouver."

"Who?"

"CSIS. Couple of people took me to a hotel room. They were pretty mad we'd run out on them in Calgary."

"So they got out the rubber hoses and you told them our whole plan?"

"No need for hoses. After all, we were going to take the videos to them afterward anyway."

"Did they give us their blessing?" I tried without success to keep the edge out of my voice.

"They were impressed that we'd found a way to get Simpson out of Seattle, but as far as they were concerned, the video idea was dumb. They really needed a more permanent solution."

"To kill Simpson?"

"They couldn't do it themselves—too many watchdogs in

the system. Libertec wanted to stay at arm's length, maybe call in an outside hit man, but that bothered the feds. So CSIS suggested that I could do it. They even gave me a weapon. I was supposed to sneak up on the cabin while you were talking to Simpson and blow him away. It would have solved our problem."

"But you didn't do it."

"I'm not the type. I wimped out, OK?"

"Why do they all want him dead?"

"Because both CSIS and the CIA have been using Libertec for contract work for years."

"And Simpson went off the rails," I said. "Maverick side deals to line his pocket, and now he's putting all their cozy relationships at risk."

"They can't just arrest him because he'll tell all."

"So they need someone to finish him off. If it isn't you, then it's got to be me, right?"

"That's what they told me yesterday."

"And that's why they hired you in the first place—in case they needed to get to me so I could help them curb Harry. Even if I thought it was a good idea, what's to say they wouldn't pin a murder charge on me afterward?"

"They'd be too afraid you'd talk. Don't worry, they promised to cover it up and nobody will come looking for you."

"Will you listen to yourself, man? We're talking about government-sanctioned murders. This isn't the sixties anymore."

Jeff stared out the front for a few seconds, then he said, "They're going to make you do it, Ben. I warned you not to leave the hospital."

"When a chance like that comes up, you take—" It suddenly came clear. "They set me up. They faked a commotion and let me escape from the hospital. So now they think they're running me as their hit man."

"They are."

"Let's see them try."

CHAPTER SEVENTEEN

I'm not sure, Ben," she said, but I knew she was my life-line so I started thinking hard as I clutched the phone receiver.

"I've always done my best for Karen," I said. "You saw what I risked to get her back when she was kidnapped."

"You know I've always trusted you with my daughter. But now you won't tell me where she is, and there was all that trouble with the video cameras—"

"I know. This must be really hard for you, but Karen's life is at risk. Mine too."

"Go to the police then," she said.

"They can't help me."

"Are you involved with the underworld?" I loved her old-fashioned language. Karen's mother, a widow now, had more spunk than anyone I knew. After her husband was killed, she'd rescued his electronics company and had gotten it back on its feet despite the devious people who had tried to control it.

"No, I haven't broken any laws."

"How much do you need?"

Relief. "Five thousand U.S. I'll make sure you get it back."

"Give me the address to wire it to."

"We can't do it that way." I gave her a phone number in Electar, the town her company runs near Kelowna, British Columbia. We were in Penticton, a city about forty miles south of Kelowna.

"So I wire the money to this person?"

"Then tell him to courier it to us here." I gave her the number to the hotel room we'd taken with virtually the last of Jeff's cash. It was a risk involving her this much, but I was hoping the FBI hadn't thought to bug her phone.

"Please let me know when you're all safe," she said.

"I will. Someday you'll know what this means to us. But don't tell anyone else. If anyone comes to see you, even from the government, tell them nothing."

"You know I'd spend any amount of money to keep my family from harm. Be careful, Ben."

"I will." She hung up, and I stared out of the dusty phone booth at the brown hills around the city. This thing would take a miracle, and I knew Karen's mom would hold me accountable.

Jeff banged on the door of the booth. "What did she say?"

"Let's get back to the hotel. I don't want to be seen on the street."

For a second I thought I saw that shifty look flash across his face again, but he'd told me all there was to tell, hadn't he? Probably not. Now that I understood my escape from the hospital was a setup, I realized they wouldn't have let me go unless they knew they had me on a leash.

What the leash was, I had no idea. Maybe a homing device on Jeff's car. Maybe they'd co-opted Jeff himself to keep them aware of where I was. We could have been followed easily from the air on our trip to Penticton and by tails on the ground once we arrived.

I had a good idea, as well, how they planned to play the next part of their plan. They'd put me into contact with Simpson in a situation where either I'd kill him or he'd kill me. I hoped they'd provide me with some sort of advantage. It didn't matter where Jeff and I holed up or how much security we used. Everything would come down to a shootout at high noon.

That evening, after we'd spent most of Jeff's last twenty bucks on supper, we sat in our hotel room and twiddled our thumbs, pretending to watch TV but really watching each other. Jeff, I thought, was probably trying to figure out how much I knew. I had only one question about him: How deep was he into the pocket of CSIS?

"Something bothering you?" he said finally.

"Why?"

"Just a chill in the room."

"No chill," I said.

"I thought we were working together on this. In fact, I don't have to be here at all."

"Sure you do. If you'd killed Simpson, your bosses wouldn't have dumped the job on me."

"Are you actually going to do it?" he asked.

"Kill Harry? Since it's government sanctioned, it's like capital punishment."

"Cut it out, Ben."

"Then don't ask questions like that."

"So what are you planning to do?"

"I'll give you the scenario. Government forces, too chicken to kill a man and loathe to arrest him for fear he'll spill the beans, these government forces let a man be kidnapped and taken to another country and put through hell. Why? Because they hope he'll draw out the bad guy or, if he survives, that he'll get mad enough to kill."

"And you're that mad right now, aren't you?"

"Could be. Does that mean I'll actually kill Harry?"

"That's what I'm asking."

"What would you do?"

"I'd wimp out. I already have."

"And then Harry would kill you. Maybe your family too. He might wait years before he jumped you. Meanwhile the feds would refuse to arrest him and would do precious little to protect you."

"If I'd killed him, I wouldn't have had any guarantee that the cops wouldn't turn on me and lock me up for life."

"Except that you'd tell all."

"So they'd have to kill me too," Jeff said.

"Bingo."

"Tell me what you're going to do."

"Sorry, Jeff. It's better if you don't know." I wasn't sure that he understood the message I was giving him.

"So you won't tell me unless..."

"Unless what?"

"Do you have a particular reason for not trusting me?"

"None," I said, my eyes wide.

"I'm on your side. I've always been." He got up quickly and left the suite. I suppose he must have gone down to the lobby for a while.

I felt guilty about the way I'd treated him, but with so many potential ears listening, there wasn't much choice. All of this would come together somewhere, and I wanted to be the one to choose the venue. A crowded shopping mall was out. So was a public street or anywhere where some poor sap walking by might take a bullet.

I phoned the nearest tourist office and told them I wanted to find an isolated hiking spot with wide vistas and terrific views. They told me about just the right place and, if our room was as bugged as I assumed it was, everybody got the same information.

The next part was more dicey. When I reached the lobby, I spotted Jeff getting into an up elevator. He pretended not to see me. I walked a couple of blocks from the hotel, feeling my skin prickle with the anticipation of having a bullet hole punched through it, but nothing stopped my progress.

I called her collect from a phone booth.

"Ben?" She started crying. "Where are you?"

"Somewhere. I can't tell you."

"Come home, please."

"We don't have a home, Karen. And if Harry gets his way and I don't do something about it, I'm going to die."

"Haven't they caught him yet?"

"They're not even trying." I told her almost everything.

"So now you're going to kill him?" she said when I'd finished. "Is he worth giving up everything you believe in?"

"As far as I'm concerned, he's a snake and a murderer. Hector's dead because of him. Who knows how many others?"

"But to kill him—"

"I'm not going to kill him."

"What then?"

"Catch him alive. Turn him over to the cops so they'll have to deal with him whether they want to or not."

"He'll kill you if he gets the chance."

"I know."

"Come home, Ben. We could disappear somewhere. My mother has lots of money to finance us."

"And then one day on some street I'll bump into someone who knows Harry."

"I'd rather have you alive now and worry about that later. Please, Ben."

"No."

"There's more to this than you've told me, isn't there? Something else is going on."

"The government agents are watching every move Jeff and I make. They're running me, and I can't get away. In fact, now they'll know where you are too, but I don't think they'll bother with you as long as I cooperate."

"You love this," she said, surprising me with the sudden anger in her voice. "The intrigue. The games."

"No."

"Little men playing cops and robbers."

"No. There isn't any choice. They won't let up on me until I deal with Harry."

"Is that what you want too, Ben? To deal with Harry?"

"I want Harry dead," I said, "but I'll settle for captured and locked up."

"And just how are you going to accomplish that?"

"I don't know—" But I did know, and it was too frightening to talk about, especially to Karen.

"Why don't you just leave it with God?"

"You think I haven't agonized over this? When I was in Central America there wasn't a minute that I didn't think about God. I know how close he was, how involved he was. That's why I'm still breathing now."

"So this is what he preserved you for, to compromise everything by going after an animal like Harry Simpson?"

"I'm not going to kill him."

"Then he's going to kill you."

I didn't say anything.

"Ben?"

"I shouldn't have called," I said.

"Why did you? What are you planning really?"

"To capture Harry."

"You can't capture Harry. You're getting ready to die, aren't you? That's why you had to call me one more time. You're going to let him kill you."

"No."

"Please, Ben!" Her voice rose to a shout, and I couldn't stand it anymore.

"I'm going to live. I love you."

"Please."

I hung up, crossed the street, watchful but seeing no one. Back to the hotel. Jeff was in the room, sitting on a chair, staring at nothing.

"Come on," I said. "We need to go for a ride."

He threw the keys to me. "Drive yourself. Over a cliff if you've got the nerve."

"No time to be miffed, Jeff," I said, tossing the keys back to him. "This is important."

He drove us out of Penticton, heading north along Okanagan Lake. No obvious surveillance, but then it wouldn't have been obvious anyway, not the way these guys were playing.

Of course, I could have been a victim of paranoia, considering that we hadn't seen even the glimmering of a sign that anyone was watching us. But I knew they wouldn't have let me escape from the hospital if they didn't have a way of keeping a close eye on us.

Early September now, and I wondered absently what Karen was planning to do for school for the kids. By now she'd have outstayed her welcome in Canada as a visitor, so she couldn't exactly enroll them in the local elementary. She'd think of something, and I found my eyes suddenly misting thinking about her having to pick up the pieces after this was over.

The view was scenic, the long hot summer having turned the almost barren hills of the Okanagan Valley to a gray-brown that contrasted sharply with the blue of Okanagan Lake, a mile-or-two-wide ribbon that ended eighty miles to the north. We spoke little, Jeff still nursing anger that I'd accused him of hiding more information, me lost in memories of my family, wondering when insanity had taken over as the main feature of my psyche.

Bottom line: I would not kill for Libertec or the FBI or the CIA or CSIS or even for myself. After that, the options died away until there was only one left. That's why Karen had begged me not to go ahead with this. She knew the way my mind worked.

We stopped at a tourist information place near Kelowna and got the data we needed, along with a map. There were two ends to the trail we were going to use, and it soon became clear that Jeff would need a mountain bike to get into position in time.

Details, maybe too many of them. Jeff had bought into the plan readily enough, and I was grateful for that. I told him so and even apologized for antagonizing him in the apartment.

We picked up a bike from a Wal-Mart. Then we headed back toward the hotel in Penticton, the bike locked to a car rack I'd bought with it.

"We'll need guns," Jeff said as we crossed the bridge out of Kelowna.

"That should be easy in Canada. All we have to do is register with the government, get a criminal record check and take a course."

"I don't care. We're going to need some serious weaponry if we're going to get out of this alive." I hoped the car wasn't bugged.

"You don't need anything," I said, "because they're not even going to see you, right?"

"That's the part I object to. I could follow them after they were past me."

"And get yourself killed."

"The feds will make sure you have a gun."

"I'll have to deal with that my own way."

"Simpson will kill you."

"Maybe. At least my family will be safe."

"You're serious about the way you want to play this? I went along because I thought you—"

"You thought I'd see how stupid it was and opt for the guns ablazing approach? Look, Jeff, I'm sorry to be giving you so much hassle, but I don't want you going down with me."

"You're my friend. What you're planning is suicide."

"Not suicide, Jeff. Insanity maybe."

Insanity for sure.

CHAPTER EIGHTEEN

H ere's the plan," I said. We were back in our hotel room, and if they hadn't bugged us by now the humiliation of talking to them as if they had would be the least of our worries.

"That's Ben speaking," Jeff said, his nerves forcing him into the world of the inane.

"We're going to set this up in Myra Canyon," I said. "That's part of the Kettle Valley Railway line that they've restored as a hiking trail. It's southeast of Kelowna. We're going to do this September 5, two days from now."

Most of the planning depended on the cops. They had to leak word to Simpson through Libertec, telling him I was hiding in Kelowna and using the canyon daily as an isolated place to work out. Simpson would have to enter the trail at its west end and hike or bicycle in so that he'd get to where I was by ten. We planned it so he'd arrive on a weekday and no one, we hoped, would be on the trail early. The cops would have to block the road access at both ends of the trail as soon as Simpson and whoever he brought with him had reached the starting point.

I even told them how to leak the news to Simpson—a carelessly left memo from one administrator in Libertec to another explaining where I was hiding and when and where I ran every-day. It would indicate that my hotel room was booked under a false name only through the fifth and the feds thought I'd be moving on after that date.

"Jeff and I will be in place in the canyon before ten. Simpson is to be given the information that I usually run only to the second tunnel from the Myra end of the trail. What he won't know is that Jeff will signal me with a cell phone and I'll be waiting to take Simpson out on his way to the tunnel.

"You people will provide a sniper style rifle for me. I want an automatic, and it had better be set up perfectly because I may have to take out several people at once."

Listen to me. If they could have known what I really intended to do, they would have stuffed me into a padded cell for three lifetimes.

"We sure hope you're getting this," Jeff added, giving me the urge to slug him.

"Whatever way you set this up," I said, "don't let Simpson enter the trail from the east end. Even if you have to fake a land-slide after we use the road. He's got to come at me from the west end so I can see him coming."

None of this would make much sense to them until they got out maps and traced the routes I'd projected. Myra Canyon was the route of a defunct rail line, now turned into a trail. From above, it looked like a rough W, the two tops of the letter forming the two ends of the trail—the former stations of Ruth on the West and Myra on the east. Each end was accessible by road from Kelowna. The bottom of the W stretched south, looping around the canyon.

The canyon itself was in mountain wilderness. Seven miles of wide trailbed, now without railway ties, hung on the edge of massive mountains, giving a spectacular view of the two-thousand-foot deep canyon below. In all, there were sixteen wooden trestles and two steel ones to span areas where there was not enough mountainside to hold the railbed. Near the Myra end were two tunnels, the second of these about a half-hour walk along the trail. That was where Simpson would probably plan to lie in wait for me if I didn't kill him first.

"You'll have to block all traffic up to both ends of the canyon once Simpson and his goons arrive. He'll probably be on the trail by eight in the morning at the latest, and then no one else goes up there. I don't want a stray bullet wiping out some hiker. Except for Simpson, of course." Careful. I was starting to feel hysteria in my voice.

"We're counting on you guys to set this up right," Jeff said. "You do your part and we'll do ours."

Jeff and I spent the afternoon shopping, money flowing like water. If I was going to die, I didn't want it said that I'd gone ill-equipped. The two of us couldn't even look each other in the eye.

Late in the afternoon, as I was walking back into a mall from adding to the pile of stuff in the car, a man in rough clothes bumped into me and shoved a piece of paper and a pill bottle into my pocket. I went to a washroom and locked myself in a stall. The note read:

Your plan accepted. Find the object near the parking area at the Myra end of the canyon. Tree will be marked with small orange star. Object will be in a case under fallen tree branches six feet behind marked tree. The rest as you laid it out.

Nothing more, not even a "good luck." The pill bottle was

my antimalarial medicine. At least I was sure now that they were running me and that I hadn't been overcome by rampant paranoia. I found Jeff and gave him the note.

"For a while there," he said, "I thought you might be wrong about them knowing where we were."

"I'm never wrong, Jeff." I tried to grin.

We caught a movie that night, some high adventure thing with lots of noise and gaping holes in the plot line. If I'd thought about it more at the time, I might have understood why the flick left me with a warm feeling. The hero survived.

We went over the gear the next morning—enough equipment to let us survive in the mountains for two weeks just in case—and packed it in the car. Though I chafed at the delay in getting to the meeting with Simpson, I knew we had to give him time to get to the canyon on the fifth.

We killed the rest of the day slowly, and I slept badly that night. Jeff in the bed opposite me thrashed for hours. Finally, when he was still for a moment, I could pray: "This isn't the way I dreamed of it ending. Harry was supposed to go down and I was supposed to survive."

I breathed in the silence.

"I never planned to kill him," I said. That's right, Ben, try to get one past God. "I did, I mean I wanted to, but I won't. Hector was the last straw. He shouldn't have died just so Harry could put a few more bucks in his pocket. Can't you—"

Can't you understand, God, the white-hot fury that comes when a man without conscience plays supreme being over the fate of someone who doesn't deserve it? Some Judas who doesn't even have a motive worth talking about and he chooses his victim by how much will be brought into his coffers.

I might have killed Harry in that moment if I'd had a chance, and it scared me badly because I thought I'd beaten the anger down to a manageable roar. I certainly didn't need to learn now how eager I was to see him die.

I heard an alarm buzzing and realized I must have slept an hour or two. Three in the morning. I woke Jeff and he got up, looking grieved in the dim light of the single lamp I'd turned on. While he showered, I ate a couple of breakfast bars we'd left in the fridge.

We were on the road at three-thirty after finishing the check-out with a bleary-eyed clerk. I drove, wanting the challenge so that I could see if the last vestiges of the malaria were going to be a problem. No sign of fever or chills.

"Go over it again," Jeff said.

"We've rehearsed it to death."

"I'm coming to you on the mountain bike from Ruth, right?"

"Ruth doesn't exist anymore."

"From the place where the Ruth train station used to operate. The west end of the canyon. Five miles or so to the tunnel, maybe six."

"You want to stop at least half a mile short of it. We've walked through this already, Jeff, and it's doing my nerves no good at all."

"Are you sure you can find the right roads?"

"I memorized the map."

Okanagan Lake was a wide ribbon to our right, but I saw it only occasionally in the dark. Memories intruded of the last time I'd been there, two years before when Jeff and I had driven to Kelowna to rescue Karen from her kidnappers. The fire I'd started.

I'd never pictured starting the last day of my life driving in the dark, reliving past nightmares. It was hardly fair that the end would come with the accompaniment of a sour stomach and a touch of headache.

We got to Kelowna at four-thirty, dawn still far off, and my mental atlas kicked in as we covered the tangle of back roads to the former terminus of Ruth. It was still dark when we arrived at the spot high in the hills. Darkness was good, since I suspected that Simpson would want to wait for sunrise before he took the route we'd followed. We got out and unstrapped Jeff's bike. I helped him load the pack on his back.

"Ready?" I said.

"You can trust me this time, Ben."

"I never doubted I could," I said. "You've told me everything?"

"Pretty well."

"Mind telling me the rest now?"

"It's getting late. I don't have anything else you should know about."

"If I were a woman, you'd probably tell me not to worry my pretty little head about details."

"You can trust me."

"I know."

I heard the words, "Lord, protect him," and realized that Jeff was praying. I'd been doing the same for a couple of hours because there was no way...

"We'll meet at the Myra end when it's over," I said. "On no account are you to come near the tunnel until I give you the OK."

"Fine, Ben. But the risk—"

"Is mine to take."

He tried to smile. "I won't let you down," he said, then he got on the bike and rode away.

I swung the car in a circle and I headed back down, following roads around the perimeter of the canyon before catching the dirt logging road that would lead me back up into the mountains to the Myra end. At the top, I nearly missed the last turnoff but spotted it just in time. There was a rough parking area, but mine was the only car.

Light was showing over the hills. I found the rifle right where the note had promised it would be, and I slung it by its strap over my shoulder. A trail led toward the canyon, which I couldn't yet see. Hurrying, I pulled my pack over my other shoulder, then thought better of it and strapped it on properly, the rifle feeling out of place and awkward. For no practical reason, I locked the car before I headed down the trail.

No one who hadn't been there before could have been prepared for the sight as I rounded a corner, the sun just up over the eastern mountains as the canyon came into view. "One of the seven natural wonders of North America," the woman at the tourism station had told me. I had no idea what the other six might be.

There was an immense chasm ringed by evergreen-covered mountains, the enormity of its size and depth taking my breath from me. For a moment I felt as though I were perched at the end of the world, in the last place of wild creation, with the sun illuminating the folds of the mountains and the mounds and crags and crevices that lined the gigantic hole below. Across it, I could see the biggest of the steel railway trestles still there after decades of defying the mind-numbing heights.

As I walked, a string of wooden trestles came into view. Each one had been planked over and had railings added, but it took little imagination to realize what would happen if one of them gave way. Where the mountainside would support it, the original railbed had been carved into the rock, tracks now long gone, leaving behind a gravel road. Where chasms made a railbed impossible, there were trestles, each revealing under them steep embankments covered with loose rock. The very bottom of the canyon was over two thousand feet down.

Fifteen minutes later I reached the first tunnel, long, a half cylinder cut roughly out of the rock, the inside face of it jagged all the way through. Sudden chill as the temperature dropped several degrees and most of the light disappeared. The tunnel took a bend and then there was light again, revealing a small rockfall that had piled a few feet of stone on the floor of the other end.

I wasn't as interested in the tunnel itself as the large rocks around its mouth that could take me up on top of it. Gingerly, I started to climb, finding my way easier than I thought I would given that my leg constantly threatened to give out on me. From above the tunnel, the view was great, the big trestle across the canyon clearly visible. Finding a dip in the ground, I burrowed down and waited.

Seven o'clock. The air was warmer now, birds singing nearby. There was some high overcast in the sky, but it looked like the day would end sunny. I felt enveloped by the mountains and trees, as if my mother had put her arms around me.

Jeff would be in place by now, burrowed in somewhere about a mile ahead, his bike, I hoped, well hidden. I knew there was probably still something left in his bag of tricks, but he knew what I wanted to do and he'd promised not to interfere.

I reminded myself that I shouldn't wait too long because I still had to get into position at the second tunnel, but this one gave me a better view of the big steel trestle. Occasionally I glanced at the rifle lying to the right of me. It had a very expensive-looking sniper scope. Simpson wasn't expecting me to be waiting in ambush, and from my vantage point I had a perfect line of fire to the trestle.

I remembered Karen saying to me on the phone, "Are you going to kill him?"

Now I wasn't sure I had an answer.

ine-thirty. It was getting warm as I sat with my back against a rock and watched the big trestle across the canyon. I'd made myself a screen out of branches so that anyone looking for me with binoculars would be out of luck. The rifle and my pack were stowed away.

"I hoped for more time," I said to God. "The past few years it seems like I've done nothing but dance on the edge of a cliff."

It had been worth it, though, coming to the end of myself, finding him waiting for me, knowing that our relationship made me alive.

"You got any last bright ideas?" I asked him. "Maybe a spare lightning bolt for when Harry crosses the trestle?"

I felt as if he were speaking to me. "Can I trust you, Ben?" he said.

"I'm here, aren't I?"

"Can I trust you?"

"I said I wouldn't kill him."

"But you're angry."

"Angry enough to kill, but I won't."

"Can I trust you?"

I leaned my head back and let the sun warm my face. A hawk was circling very high, watching for movement below, and I thought about the fact that surprise is the primary weapon of the predator. If I saw him on the trestle across the chasm and I used the scope, I could pick him off right there, far away from me. Like a bolt out of heaven.

In many places in the world, the state would have executed a Harry Simpson. Hadn't the state already made me its agent, even handed me the gun?

Can I trust—

O Lord, how I wanted to raise the gun and see him in the sights and pull the trigger myself and watch him stagger back under the impact of the bullet, watch him teeter at the railing then plunge, screaming, into the void. But I couldn't imagine God applauding in the wings while I vented my rage on Harry Simpson.

"Yes," I said to him, "you can trust me. I won't kill him, but I might go to my grave wishing I had. What does that make me?"

Human. Fallen for sure. Endlessly capable of living out the permutations of my depravity. But for the grace of God, I would have rejoiced to pull the trigger. The thought is as bad as the deed, I'd heard a pastor say. Jesus taught much the same in the Sermon on the Mount. What did that make me?

Cell phone. The sudden shrill tone in this divine cathedral almost shot my heart out of my chest.

"You there?" Jeff said.

"Waiting at the first tunnel for sight of him."

"I'm here. Fully in place."

"Fine." I terminated the call.

Probably just feeling lonely. He knew where I'd be and I knew where he'd be. Almost ten and no sign of Harry. I couldn't blame Jeff for thinking we were the last two people on earth. The canyon had such power to overwhelm you and blot out all other possible horizons.

Then I saw a flicker of movement on the trestle across the canyon. Someone on a bike, then two of them, three. Carefully I reached back for the rifle, found it, sheltered it under my canopy of branches so that it wouldn't reflect the sun, pointed.

Through the scope I saw Harry Simpson, his two men behind him. They were riding steadily despite the warning that bicycles should be walked across the trestles. I wondered what the distance was, suspected that the rifle could cover it without much drop in trajectory.

Then I put it down because the temptation was getting to me, and I'd seen everything I needed to. Harry would have to fall over the edge on his own.

Cell phone. "I have them in sight now, Ben."

"Can you see what weapons they're packing?"

"Probably just handguns. If they're planning to wait for you in the tunnel, they only need short-range stuff."

"How long before they reach ground zero?"

"Don't call it that. Maybe fifteen minutes. You better get into position."

"All right, Mommy," I said.

"Ben?"

"Yeah."

"You could still do this another way."

"That's what I've done all my life."

"They're going to kill you."

"I appreciate the vote of confidence. Maybe they won't."

"I'll explain it to Karen if you don't make it."

"Thank you, Mr. Morbid."

"If I...if I found some way for backup—"

"No, Jeff."

"But if I—"

"No. Thanks for all you've done, but this one will be just me and Harry."

"And the two guys he brought with him."

"They'll do what he tells them. Look, I've got to go. Thanks again for everything."

I disconnected and gathered my stuff, worried now that I'd left it too long. Climbing down would have been harder than going up, but with the rifle and pack well hidden behind me, I had less to tote around. I reached the trail quickly and followed it around the several bends and over more trestles leading to the second tunnel, its facade cemented into a smooth mantle with rough rock face further in.

This needed thinking about. If I surprised them, they'd shoot without hesitation. If I gave them too much chance to look me over they'd shoot me from a distance before I could talk to them.

No time left. I walked through the tunnel, then climbed up above it from the other end, stopping about twenty feet up. A jagged boulder shielded me from view. Finally I heard scrunching sounds—tires on gravel—coming up fast. I almost acted too soon, but I hung on, waiting, until they were right there.

"Harry!"

Sudden braking. "Where are you, Ben?" Was he afraid? Did he think I'd gotten the jump on him?

"We have to talk."

Then they homed in on my voice and someone started shooting until Simpson told him to knock it off.

"Are you armed?" Harry asked.

"Rifle with a scope. But I left it somewhere else."

"What are you trying to pull?"

"I could have killed all of you when you crossed the big trestle. I didn't do it. In fact, I'm trying to save your life."

"And I came all this way to kill you. So where does that leave us?"

"Why don't you kill me, then," I said, standing up, the top half of my body exposed. "You'll die too, but if that's your pleasure…"

He raised his pistol and I saw that it had a silencer screwed on.

"Those silencers are murder on proper gun performance," I said to him.

"Don't start irritating me, Ben. I'd rather you gave me three excellent reasons not to blow your head off."

"Number one," I said, "how did Libertec know where I was so they could leak the information to you? Number two, how did I know you were coming so I could ambush you if I wanted to? Number three, where did I get a high-powered rifle with a scope? You should see the thing, Harry. It's a real beauty."

"And the answers?"

"Only one answer—the whole of western intelligence has sucked you into a trap, and I'm the executioner."

"What's wrong with you then? Lost your nerve? Lost your brains? If you could have killed me on the trestle, why didn't you?"

"Because I hate you too much, Harry, and I don't want you dead before I learn how to deal with it."

"You make no sense at all, Ben."

"Nothing good makes sense to an evil man."

I didn't see him coming. He came out of the bush and down onto the railbed fifty feet behind Harry and his friends, who were still staring at me. Jeff had an automatic rifle.

"Where did you get that?" I asked.

"Get what?" Simpson said.

Jeff said nothing.

"Don't do anything sudden, Harry," I said, "but if you'll look behind you, you'll see how truly doomed you are."

He turned, and I fully expected Jeff to open fire. But he just held his rifle steady at shoulder height.

"Guns over the side," he said. They hesitated, then obliged, three small black objects sailing out into the void.

"How did the feds talk you into this?" I asked Jeff.

"Didn't have to." He walked closer, gun still ready for firing. "What were your odds, Ben? Fifty-fifty that Harry wouldn't kill you right off? Ten percent that he'd turn himself in?"

"I was ready to die. At least Karen and the kids would have been safe when Harry got his pound of flesh. So what did you tell them?"

"Who?"

"Your pals at CSIS. They gave you a gun."

"I said I thought you'd chicken out, but I'd be glad to do the job myself. I told them I was embarrassed that I failed the last time up at Harrison Lake."

"Is this getting through to you, Harry?" I asked. "They want you dead—Libertec, CSIS, the FBI, the CIA. Above all, they don't want you telling the world about—"

"Get it over with," he said. "I'd prefer a quick head shot, if you don't mind."

"Too easy," Jeff said. "I didn't come for you anyway, just for your henchmen. If I turn you in to the feds, they'll be mighty displeased that you're breathing." He waved the end of his rifle at Harry's goons and backed up to the edge of the trail. "Move. If you get closer than ten feet from me, I'll kill you." They did what they were told, passing him uneasily and then stopping to wait for orders.

"What about Harry?" I said.

"I told the cops we'd hide the bodies and I'd bring you back out the way I came," Jeff said. "As far as I know, no one's hanging around your car at this end."

"They've blocked the roads."

"No worries." He fired three times into the air, waited a few seconds, then took out his cell phone and dialed awkwardly, still pointing the rifle. "It's done," he said into the phone. "Give us half an hour then open up the roadblocks and clear out."

"This wasn't in the plan, Jeff."

"Your plan was stupid. Did I do good?"

"You did good."

"I'll be waiting for you where Karen's staying. What's your next move?"

"Just tell her we'll all be safe soon."

He motioned his two captives to move, and they went down the trail. From what I could see, he'd have some explaining to do to the cops unless he shed himself of Harry's men before he went back to town. In his shoes, that's exactly what I'd do. He could pick up his bike on the way back, march the bad guys out of the canyon and then leave them on foot at the other end.

Harry was standing at the entrance of the tunnel, his face revealing nothing. I wondered if he might be tempted to bash my head in with a rock and run for it.

"I chucked my rifle," I said. "Maybe we should go to the nearest trestle and fight it out until one of us goes over, just like in the movies."

He scowled.

"You can go, Harry. Just leave. I don't have the energy to

hog-tie you and drag you to the cops. And they don't want to see you alive anyway. The original plan was to convince you that the game was up. It is, you know. If that didn't work, you'd kill me and my family would be safe. If you believed me, I'd take you to a newspaper reporter so the feds would be less inclined to dispose of you when you turned yourself in. Prison's better than execution, after all."

"I could still kill you, Ben."

"What for? To shut me up? Every fed in the world knows already, and it was Libertec that set you up to walk into my trap."

"Revenge is a good motive."

"Grow up. Your choices are two right now: turn yourself in or flee to Pago Pago. In either case, killing me will only make the cops more hungry to finish you off."

He smiled without humor. "Your friend Jeff is a devious character, isn't he? With his cell phone he could arrange for just about anything."

"Afraid someone's going to pop you the minute we separate?"

"All I've got for transportation is a bike. Even a four-year-old with a gun could take me out on my way back to town."

"I hope he does. So long, Harry." I started into the tunnel.

"Wait a second," he said. I stopped. "Explain the other option."

"We drive to the newspaper office in Kelowna and you tell a reporter who you are and what you're alleged to have done. He calls the police and you go meekly into a cell."

"Why the middleman?"

"Don't be dense, Harry. The feds want you dead. You need an independent witness who can tell the world that you went into custody alive."

"You could've killed me."

"I hate you too much for that. When this is over, I've still got to work my attitude out with God."

He looked at me as if I were an idiot.

"You've got plenty of reason to hate me," he said.

"Not to kill you."

"Maybe that will change," he said, turning and walking just ahead of me through the cold tunnel.

We saw no one during the half-hour trek back to my car. The parking area was deserted.

Being extra cautious now, I didn't take the route I'd come up on, opting for the longer road that wound down to McCullough and then a secondary highway back to Kelowna.

A few miles from the newspaper office, I said to Harry, "You realize that you've run out of options."

"Appears so."

"Don't give me any trouble when we arrive."

"Trouble's already here," he said, and I felt the point of something sharp poking into my ribs.

CHAPTER TWENTY

I hadn't started with much hope and maybe that's what had made me careless when I should have tied Harry's hands to the car doorpost or at least frisked him. He'd caved in on me in Myra Canyon, and I thought God had come through in an enormous way. But God hadn't counseled me to toss away my brains.

Simpson made me drive to the bus station on the edge of Kelowna where he picked up a parcel under a false ID, shipped from Vancouver. I stood beside him, speechless, while he collected it with his right hand and kept the knife palmed in his left, its point pressing against my ribs.

"What have you got?" I said when we were back inside the car. He unwrapped it—a tiny .22 pistol.

"Backup," he murmured.

"You must have found yourself a network," I said.

"Not much. I like to work alone and buy the help I need."

"Who sent you the gun?"

He didn't answer.

He made me park on a quiet side street and walk with him the half mile to a seedy motel outside the tourist fringe. Any thought of running from him was dismissed by my limp. I was no candidate for a footrace with someone as fit and strong as Harry Simpson.

While we stood at the counter in front of some tired and underpaid clerk, it came to me that Harry had worked out a full alternate scenario. Since he had no idea what Jeff might have told the cops, he was going to Plan B.

"Name?"

"Gus Johnson," Harry said. "I'm paying."

"Him?"

"Ben Sylvester," I said, knowing that Harry could have let loose a bloodbath right there.

"It's on my tab, not his," Harry said quickly.

"You can call me Ben," I said, putting out my hand.

Once in the room, a reasonably sized twin on the third floor, with bolted down TV and kitchenette, Harry dragged a pair of handcuffs out of his pocket.

"Give it a rest," I said. "You've got me, OK? I'm too tired to do anything but be your meek little hostage."

He said nothing, just pointed the gun and made me lock my right arm to the headboard of one of the beds. I decided to lie down.

"This has been done before, you know," I said. "After a while somebody figures things out and then the cops start banging on the door and you shout, 'No closer or Sylvester gets it,' and then you tell them your demands and the cops weigh you down with delays until you get sleepy and make a mistake."

"That was always the thing about you that got to me the most, Ben—your smart mouth. For a while you were the best field man Libertec ever had, but it was all I could take to be in the same room with you."

"I'm like a cat, Harry. They always notice when something's starting to smell and then they pounce on it. I smelled you from the first. That's why I ragged you so much."

"Come off it. You never suspected me of anything. You were always pretty stupid about duplicity."

I closed my eyes. "What's your big plan now, Harry? You could have been miles from here if you'd told me to keep on driving."

"Everything's on track, Ben."

"And you're not going to tell me."

"If you knew the number of times I was tempted to shoot you in the past couple of years..."

"Tell me why you chose me to be the victim of your greedy schemes after you went bad."

"I never went bad. I just got smarter."

"Don't patronize me."

"Don't act like it's your right to know everything, Ben."

"I didn't kill you up there in the canyon, even when I had a bead on you through my scope. That's worth something."

"A merit badge for stupidity?" He sat down on the edge of his bed and pointed his gun, two-handed, at my head. I saw sudden rage on his face, and I braced myself. Then he put the gun on his lap, his hand still holding it. "So sanctimonious, Ben. So right all the time. So much smarter than everybody else."

"If you're that angry, I'm surprised you didn't kill me before we got here," I said.

"Not yet. I still need a hostage." I didn't like the way his lips worked themselves into a smile. "Have you grasped it yet that I beat you? I outsmarted you all the way down the line."

"Not too likely, Harry."

"Your big mouth started the operation that got your wife kidnapped, Ben," he said. "I overheard you in the cafeteria grousing about your father-in-law, the big electronics magnate who loved to terrorize his wife and daughter. It seemed to me like a perfect setup to generate money."

"You set up a spy ring in my father-in-law's company, then something went wrong and your Middle Eastern contacts started calling the shots. When my father-in-law launched his own investigation, you knew the whole thing was in trouble."

"Good, Ben. That's when I hired someone to take you out during a fake mission I sent you on, and I arranged for Karen to be kidnapped to keep her old man quiet."

"So quiet he's six feet under."

"Why so calm, Ben? Why aren't you foaming at the mouth?"

"Because it would make you happy." My pulse was going too fast, and I knew that if I didn't do some deep breathing I'd start screaming. "Did Libertec OK all this?"

"They gave me a free hand. I caught a little flak later, but nothing too bad. Saluso was more of a problem. We sent you to Africa knowing full well he was planning a coup, but we really expected him to make a better show of it. My bosses weren't at all happy with me."

"Didn't you ever worry about me, Harry? Or my family?"

"You think I enjoyed sending you out there?"

"Yes," I said, returning his stare. "If I'm understanding you so far, you were working more or less under the orders of Libertec, though I realize the FBI and CIA were part of a lot of your operations. When did you go freelance?"

"Who says I did?"

"Why does Libertec want you dead, then?"

"Because I've been skimming their profits."

"What about Juanita and Hector?"

"The president wanted somebody to train a team to organize

the next election. You spotted the fake right away, so when you got back and told us about the guerrillas who'd helped you escape, I went down there and found Hector."

"How did you do that when even the Juanitan army couldn't?"

"Who cares?"

"You contacted the CIA, didn't you? They told you." He didn't answer. "And you told Hector there was no hope of a fair election, so he might as well buy some arms."

"Actually, he'd already seen the lay of the land and was looking for a seller. He even had a lot of cash raised. But there was a goof-up and Libertec found out I skimmed ten thousand of it." He paused. "Look, I'm fed up with them, OK? Stupid little exploits tinkering with balances of power. What does it mean anyway? People get the rulers they deserve."

"A twinge of guilt, Harry? Let me guess: Libertec took your ten thousand so you made up for your loss by selling Hector to the Juanitan president."

He said nothing.

"They want you dead, Harry. You went freelance on Libertec and you betrayed Hector, the guy the CIA was backing."

"Doesn't matter. I'm leaving soon and I've got plenty to live on."

"What was your impression of Hector, Harry?" I could hardly breathe now.

"Another dumb revolutionary. Things were better in the old days when all of them were Marxists. At least they had a philosophy instead of this bleeding-heart give-us-freedom junk."

"You're the one who made him a revolutionary by selling him the guns. Do you have any idea about the human rights abuses in Juanita? Did you even check out what you were dealing with before you told Hector that guns were his only hope?"

"He would've bought them from somebody else if I hadn't been there. The guy was hungry."

"And then you skimmed his fee and ended up selling out a good man for money. A dog would have been more loyal."

He jumped to his feet, lunged for me, got my throat with one hand, and I couldn't fight him shackled to the bed.

But I got my left arm around the back of his head when he came in close and I squeezed hard until I saw pinwheels dancing around me, then I brought up a leg and shoved him back.

"You sold him out," I said, my voice rasping, breathing hard. "He walked right into an ambush and they slaughtered him."

He went over to his bed, picked up his little gun, pointed it at me again.

"Sign of inadequacy, Harry, using a gun on a defenseless man."

"Shut up."

"I wish I would've killed you. God said Abel's blood cried out from the ground for justice after Cain murdered him. You hear Hector's blood, Harry? Do you hear it?"

"Shut up!"

The phone rang. Harry turned toward it, then back to me. When it rang again, he picked it up. "Yes?"

He listened in silence for a couple of minutes, his pistol hanging from his hand. Then he hung up, his anger dissolving into a grin.

"Your idiot friend, Ben, what's his name—Jim?"

"Jeff."

"My guys had a spare gun hidden at the other end of the canyon. One of them tripped and came up with the gun. Your pal froze and took a bullet. Fell down a hill."

"Dead?"

"Who cares?"

I felt my last strength washing out of me, and I put my head back on the pillow. "He wasn't supposed to be part of this. What kind of—"

"Cut the grandstanding, Ben, it's time to go. This spot was only supposed to be a rendezvous."

"Where we going?"

He undid the handcuffs too quickly for me to catch him off guard and then marched me out the door, down the hall and out the fire escape stairs to the parking lot. His men were waiting by his car.

Harry turned to me. "Game over, Ben."

CHAPTER TWENTY-ONE

I got into the car, praying very hard. One of Harry's men got into the back seat with me. The other drove while Harry took his gun from him and pointed it at me from the front passenger seat.

"You should've killed me, Ben," he said as we drove away from the motel.

"And now you're going to kill me?"

"What a sap you are. This religion junk has turned you into a daisy."

"Because I didn't kill you? At least I know where I'm going when I die. You don't."

"I'm not going to die."

"So where are we headed this time, Harry?"

"Into the woods for the day. None of your business after that."

"I saved your life."

"You lacked the guts to pull the trigger. There's a difference."

"Where you planning to hide for the rest of your life, Harry?" I asked.

"Anywhere I please. I know so much the feds would never

dream of trying to pick me up."

"They could kill you."

"Sure, that's why they sent you to do it for them. They didn't have a marksman of their own handy. Look, Ben, they know I'll leave information time bombs behind that will lead the press right into their sorry little mess if I get taken out."

"Maybe they don't care anymore. Maybe taking you out is more important to them than your time bombs."

"Yeah, right." I could see the anger again, the desire to show off his superiority.

"Why bring me along then?" I said. "The cops are only just now finding out that you're still alive. You can probably get clear without dragging me along."

He smiled into my face and for the first time I could see how much he loathed me. "You sold me out, Ben."

"They've been on to you for a long time."

"You spilled your guts about me to that embassy down south. No one was trying to kill me until you released information outside the loop."

"What loop?"

"Libertec's work with the government was strictly need-to-know. You blurted it out to people who weren't in the information loop. Now I'm the fall guy so Libertec can tell everyone it's cleaned house."

"You're wrong. They want you because you're a renegade. They knew about that long before I did."

"Why didn't they take me out earlier then?"

"They're all afraid of you, of what you know. They're scared that if one of them sets up a hit, it'll come back on them. That's why they tried to force me to do it."

"They tried to make you do it because you're the one who

told the wrong people about me."

"Believe what you want."

We were headed east on Highway 33 and it suddenly came to me why I was riding in Harry's car. "The lust for revenge can get in the way of common sense," I said.

"Not if you're careful. In this case, poetic justice makes real sense, Ben. I get set up for a fall, so you get set up for a fall."

We passed through the town center of Rutland. I could have tried to bolt at an intersection, but I knew Simpson would only move up the timetable for my execution and then make his getaway.

The car climbed into the hills until eventually forested mountains closed in around us. We turned up a logging road, followed it for a few miles until we found a clearing half-hidden in the trees. Simpson told his man to park behind some bushes. Big tree branches hung down everywhere, limiting our own view to a couple of hundred yards.

"Get out," Simpson told me.

"I know what you're planning," I said.

"Just get out."

"Can you give me some warning before you do it?"

"Why, so you can pray for help? Make your peace?"

I got out and sat on a nearby log. The three of them moved within ten feet of me, each choosing a tree to sit under. I was very aware of their guns.

"You don't like my faith much, do you, Harry?"

"I don't understand it. There was a time when I thought we could bring you into the inner sanctum at Libertec. You could have made some serious money."

"I'd still have to live with myself."

"Well you won't have to worry about that much longer."

"How are you going to do it?" He only grinned. "How long do I have?"

"Take the day, Ben."

I tuned him out then. It seemed to me he had a plan that was smart enough to work. At least Karen and the boys would be safe once Simpson had his revenge on me and left the scene.

He must have arranged for some sort of pick-up. If the cops had found Jeff, the discovery would set loose a pretty big manhunt. Or maybe not. Maybe Simpson was protected by a hands-off order. Maybe the feds would be happier with Harry out of the scene, hiding somewhere with his dirty secrets.

Why were we spending the day waiting in the woods? Probably because Simpson preferred darkness for whatever he was planning.

About noon, Harry's men left in the car. When they were gone, I said to him, "I want to know what drives you, Harry, what sent you down this path."

"Same as anyone—some security, some excitement, maybe a chance to make an impact."

"You never married and I've never heard you talk about relatives. So who's your life for?"

"Me, Ben. You sanctimonious family men keep holding forth about your responsibility for your loved ones. But when it comes down to a moment like this, the only one you're pulling for is yourself."

"'I see' said the blind man."

"The main reason the company hired you was that we saw a man we thought would never stop working the angles. You came across like a guy who'd be open to anything as long as it gave you power or money."

"That's not who I am anymore. Maybe I never was."

"You remember a conversation about three years ago?" he said. "We'd been contacted by some Kurdish ex-pats, but it was plain we had nothing to offer them because nobody was going to let them have a homeland or any kind of say in a democratic process. I suggested to you that we might be able to offer their people back home some arms, some military training."

"And I told you that was the best way to put the Kurds in the sewer."

"We never followed up on it because too many other people were trying to do the same. But that conversation marked the moment when we realized how wrong we'd been about you. You're a blockhead, Ben. You march to the beat of only one drummer even if he's playing the wrong song. You're heading north and the parade's heading south."

"Keen use of metaphor, Harry," I said.

"We decided not to bring you into our secret world at Libertec."

"I wouldn't have gone even if you offered."

"And this religion kick sealed it for us."

"This religion kick saved your life in Myra Canyon. I suppose you still think it made me wimpy."

"You blew your best chance to kill me."

"That wasn't wimpy, believe me."

"You're so stupid, Ben, even my dog could teach you tricks."

"Let me tell you what I am, Harry. I'm somebody who learned his limits, somebody who found forgiveness. When you terminate me, I know exactly where I'm going. You don't."

"Sure I do. It's not where you're going, believe me."

"Don't lay any bets on that, Harry. So tell me, what kind of contribution do you think you've made to the world?"

"Why does it need a contribution? I lived smart. If I made a little cash on the side—"

"Then Hector, all covered with blood, will rise out of his grave and spit in your face."

He tensed and I felt the sudden chill, cold like a clammy day with lightning on the horizon.

"Hector was out of his element," he said finally, his voice surprisingly calm. "If you're clumsy, you shouldn't play near the fire."

"Cute little proverbs don't make a very good blanket for treachery, Harry."

"Give it a rest. I wouldn't have done it if Libertec hadn't grabbed my cut."

"Your crooked cut."

"I'm amazed, Ben, that you're so spunky. Why aren't you groveling?"

"Is that what you'd prefer? I'm wondering why you're so keen on conversation with a probable dead man."

"Just passing time."

Most of it was bravado, my heart hammering my chest to pieces. But I was starting to feel ready for this.

"Are you going to tell me when and where?" I asked him.

"No."

"I hope God has as much mercy on your soul as I've had."

"I don't need mercy."

For a few seconds I stared at him, looking for a sign of guilt or dread or even uncertainty.

"It wasn't me who sold you out," I said. "You've been skimming profits and making deals with the wrong people. They were on to you before I was. That's why you're running for your life now."

"Not running, just retiring," he said. "Too bad you won't be around to do the same."

Harry's men came back a couple of hours later with salami subs, drinks, and some other packages in a cardboard box. Harry just kept staring at me with a hungry predator look on his face.

CHAPTER TWENTY-TWO

They didn't speak to me or tell me where they were going as we rode up the rough gravel road in the darkness. But it soon became obvious because I'd been on this road before, very recently in fact. The road to Myra Canyon.

Give Harry an A for cunning. After all the planning the feds had done for me to kill Simpson in the canyon, they'd packed up and gone wherever feds go. But Harry had seen its potential for what I supposed would be an airlift. As one last nasty joke, Harry would probably leave my body behind where his should have been and take a sky ride to any place he wanted.

We got to the parking area and started walking, flashlights passed around to everyone but me. The beams of light formed narrow tunnels in the utter darkness, all of us walking carefully because we remembered the chasm only a few feet to our right. What had been a place of amazement in the daylight now took on sinister tones.

"Watch your step, Ben," Simpson said as I tripped over a loose rock.

"Why should you worry?"

"I don't want you slowing us down. All of this is timed out."

"Did you leave an extra few minutes for my limp?"

Harry snorted, and we said little after that, crossing trestle after trestle, navigating the two tunnels with their rough floors and plenty of loose stones. Moving around sharp bends in the trackless railbed, heading toward the big steel bridge that dominated the south side of the canyon.

"What's it going to be, Harry?" I said finally. "Chopper lift?"

"Good for you, Ben." He was slightly ahead of me, his two toughs behind me. My mind had several times evoked the vision of pushing Simpson into the canyon.

"You leave and I get to take a dive," I said.

"That's what I prefer. Of course, if you start to balk, any place along here would do just as well."

"You know, Harry, I bet I remind you of someone. Someone who died down in Central America because you sold him to his enemies. I bet every time you look at me or even think of me you see poor dead Hector. Pretty good trick if you can push me off a bridge and get rid of a ghost at the same time."

"Shut up."

"One more thing and I will. You're still mystified, aren't you, about the reason I didn't blow you away when I had the chance."

"I just put it down to stupidity."

"Let me tell you why I didn't shoot you."

"It doesn't matter now, Ben."

"Your funeral," I said.

I wasn't even sure what I'd planned to say to him. That I'd decided to live by principle? That I loved God far too much to take the life of one of his creatures no matter how dirty the guy was? That I was afraid of my anger, afraid of what it might make me if I gave in to it?

We walked in silence, the three flashlights our only source of illumination, high cloud blotting out the moon and the stars. We might as well have been at the end of the world.

It was plain to me that I was still in denial, the condemned man walking his last mile as if it meant little to him. I wondered if I'd wake up the second before they threw me off the trestle and start screaming.

Maybe it was better this way, numb and refusing to let my mind accept that my body would soon be little more than broken pulp. I knew it with my head, but it was as if the truth were locked away from me, as if I were watching it on TV and it was some other poor fool, not me.

"Hurry up, Ben," Simpson said.

"You're not the one with the limp, Harry."

"If you'd done what Saluso told you to do, he wouldn't have gotten mad enough to shoot you."

"Don't you ever, Harry. Don't you ever blame me for the evil you've brought down on me and the people I love. Don't you dare try to justify what you're doing by making me the goat."

He whirled and pointed the flashlight at my face, the beam so powerful my eyes started to water. But he said nothing. After a few seconds, he turned and carried on walking, still ahead of me, blazing the trail.

The big steel trestle, the longest one in the canyon, came far too soon, and I shuddered as Harry's flashlight picked it out, the light beam lost in the distance, unable to illuminate the other end.

Harry plunged ahead, apparently assuming his men would force me onto the trestle if I balked. I didn't balk, but my heart started betraying my fear to me, my palms wet, my bloodstream charged with surging chemicals.

We stopped near the middle, no one saying anything. At first there was only silence, then I heard the distant sound of a helicopter in flight. It came closer, but I saw nothing even when I could clearly hear the drumming of its rotors.

I'd meant to ask Harry how he'd managed to hire a helicopter to do a job like this, but I guess money talks loud enough to buy just about anything. Maybe his spy network at Electar, soon to be shut down for good, had a pilot in its pocket.

The noise was incredible now, and Harry shot the beam upward to reveal the dark shape of a small chopper maybe fifty feet above us, air rushing down hard on us from its blades.

Then he shined the flashlight on me and started waving the beam away from me to the chasm beyond the railing and back again. The message was unmistakable. I shook my head.

He walked right up to me, stuck his face inches from mine and shouted something. I couldn't hear him. He grabbed my sleeve and pulled me toward the railing. I resisted and finally broke loose. I used my hand to pantomime someone shooting me in the head, because I wanted it to be quick if he was going to finish me anyway.

I suppose he could have delegated one of his men to do it, but something you could always say about Harry Simpson was that he took his own responsibilities seriously. Raising the pistol, he pointed it at me from two feet away.

I turned and started walking away from him, wondering which one would be the last step.

A shot, barely heard above the roar of the chopper. Another and another. Somehow I'd expected that I'd feel the concussion more. Slowly I sank to my knees, a final benediction to a life that had been too short, too nasty. I didn't feel any pain at all. None, and then I realized I was still kneeling. Three bullets in me, and I wasn't flat on my face, breathing my last?

Behind me, the chopper suddenly flew off, the roar evaporating into blessed peace. I was grateful that Harry had given me a few final moments of silence, there on the big steel trestle in the amazing canyon, to commune with the One who had shaped this place with his hands just as surely as he had built the place to which I was going.

Silence, and I opened my eyes. I was still kneeling there, feeling a bit winded but maybe strong enough to stand up. No pain.

Slowly I stood and turned. Darkness. I couldn't see a thing. Maybe they'd left a flashlight behind. I walked back toward the middle of the trestle and stumbled over something big lying on the planking. Reaching down, I felt what seemed to be an arm, a torso. My hand was wet. Fumbling, I found a flashlight and struggled to turn it on. Body of one of Harry's men. I shone the light farther along the trestle and picked out the body of the other goon, then a little farther, Harry Simpson. I ran forward, checked for pulses. None.

Harry lay on his back, his eyes wide, a large stain on his chest, his face calm as if his mind never registered the sudden change in circumstances. His gun was still in his hand, and by some stupid reflex I grabbed it and threw it over the railing. I didn't hear it land.

"Ben Sylvester!" Bullhorn from the hillside to the west at the far end of the trestle. "There's nothing for you here. Get up and walk out the way you came."

I cupped my hands and shouted back, "Do you feel better now?"

I started walking, understanding then that I was OK, that the only thing about me that hurt was my leg. Behind me, finally harmless, lay the man I hadn't killed.

May God give you justice, Harry Simpson.

CHAPTER TWENTY-THREE

The people who killed Harry let me go. They let me walk out of the canyon, my leg screaming at me. I didn't know if they were from Libertec or the government, so every step I took I waited for the bullet that would take me out as cleanly as it had done Harry. No shot came, and no one was waiting for me at the other end. I hadn't thought to take the car keys from the dead driver's pocket. I just kept on walking down the winding dirt road until a police car came along.

The cop drove me to the bus depot in Kelowna. The first thing I asked him was what he knew about Jeff. He told me an ambulance had taken him to the hospital and he'd been flown from there to Vancouver. No word on his condition. I took the first bus back to Mission after I'd called Karen.

"It's over," I told her.

"You killed him?"

"No. I said I wouldn't."

"Is he dead?"

"Yes."

"Who did it?"

"I don't know."

"You're not hurt?"

"I'm fine. We'll talk when I get there. Have you heard anything about Jeff?"

"Somebody shot him in the shoulder. He's in Vancouver Hospital for an operation, but they say he'll be all right."

I exhaled.

"When are you coming?"

"Meet me at the Abbotsford Greyhound station at three."

"Ben?"

"We'll talk then."

I needed the bus trip. While I was buying the ticket my head started pounding so hard I thought it would explode. Ben Sylvester on overload couldn't have been a pretty sight, and a day's travel in the mountains wouldn't hurt.

No one sat beside me on the bus, maybe because I reeked of trauma. I put my head back and watched the rolling hills, covered with trees once we'd climbed out of the dry Okanagan Valley, and I felt as if I were absorbing God's creation through my skin.

For a while I could scarcely put two thoughts together, then after a lunch stop and more mountains, I started letting the whole story play itself through my brain. Perhaps I lacked the strength to turn it off. When it was almost over and I saw myself walking off the big trestle with Harry on the ground behind me, my cheeks were wet and I knew I was more tired than I'd ever been before.

There are some who would put all their experiences into boxes, each with a label, tidy and well defined. But experience is resistant to categories, to easy explanation.

Had I succeeded or failed? I didn't kill Harry, though the lust I'd felt for his warm blood had been virtually unstoppable. But I'd operated by a bold and stupid plan all on my own just as I'd been doing all my life, and but for the grace of God I would have been lying at the bottom of Myra Canyon.

When the bus got to Abbotsford, the closest terminal to Mission, Karen and the boys were waiting along with Dave. I felt such a rush of life when I saw them that I wondered how my flesh and bones could contain it.

We hugged and cried. I looked into Karen's face and saw welcome there, and pain. Not anger.

"Are you sure you're all right?" she asked me.

"Not a scratch."

I scooped up Jimmie and put an arm around Jack. "How was it in the war, Dad?" Jimmie asked.

"Not fun," I said. "It's better to be back here where I don't have to fight any more wars."

"Is that true, Dad?" Jack asked. "No more?"

"No more."

Later, after we'd stopped for a meal at Dave Mancuso's house, and after I'd gone to the hospital to see Jeff, Karen and I could talk about it.

"You risked everything so that Harry would at least leave the kids and me alone," she said as we lay in our room.

"Yes."

"Did you think that after you were gone we'd spend the rest of our lives thanking you for your sacrifice?"

"I don't know."

"We're a family, Ben. You don't sacrifice one part to protect another."

"You said I did it because I loved the challenge. Cops and robbers."

"I was angry."

"And now?"

"I don't think I'd have been able to bear it if you'd killed him, or he killed you."

"It was only the grace of God. I don't want you ever to let me boast about it."

"What are we going to do now, Ben?"

"Now is the hardest part of all—we have to leave everything behind."

"We've already done that."

"They let me go," I said. "You need to understand this, Karen—they let me go but I don't know when or if they'll decide it was a bad idea."

She tried to mask her fear. "What do you mean? What more could they possibly want from you?"

I lay back on the bed and closed my eyes. "Our government used Libertec to do its dirty work. I know a lot and I'll probably figure out more. Libertec's probably lost any future contracts with the feds and some government spy chief might decide around election time that I'm a liability. There are just too many variables."

"Are you saying we're going to have to disappear?"

"That's what I'm saying. When I phoned your mom earlier, she said she'd pay anything to have us kept safe. She can get us started and we'll pay her back one day."

"Where?"

"I don't know. Somewhere. It's no guarantee, but we have to do something."

"Go to the newspapers and tell them everything you know."

"That would've worked if I had Simpson in tow. Without him I've got nothing but a wild story. Did you hear any news about three bodies in Myra Canyon?"

"No."

"And you won't."

"I can't just…this is…" There were tears on her face.

"I'm sorry," I said. "I never meant it to fall apart like this."

"You're the bravest man I know, Ben."

"Where did that come from?"

"I'll go anywhere with you."

"The kids?"

"They'll adapt. We'll find a new life."

"Don't go all Pollyanna on me. We're in for grim times."

"But you didn't kill him. You stood fast. That's worth something." She reached over and touched my face.

"God hasn't given us a road map," I said.

"We don't need one."

Jeff decided to go back to Bellingham and pick up the library job he left so long before. So far nobody has come after him. For ourselves, writing it all down has been therapeutic.

I still sometimes feel the need to make sense of it, to package it in neat categories, to say, "Here I was right and there I was wrong." But the urge is not as strong now, and maybe that's good.

We've found a new home and a new life. The one Constant is there, and when we're baffled, we remember that he's all we ever wanted.

William Badke is associate professor of Bible and Theology at Northwest Baptist Theological College and Seminary in Langley, British Columbia, where he also serves as librarian of the Associated Canadian Theological Schools. He can be reached via e-mail at: badke@twu.ca.